DEATH IN

C000319015

Nancy Livingston was ~~~~
Tees. She has worked as an actress, an air
stewardess and a TV production assistant. Her
radio plays have been broadcast in Great
Britain and abroad, and she has written three
sagas: *The Far Side of the Hill*, *The Land of Our
Dreams*, and *Never Were Such Times*. Gollancz
has published all seven of Nancy Livingston's
crime novels: *Trouble at Aquitaine* (winner of
the Crime Writers' Association Poisoned Chal-
ice Award), *Fatality at Bath & Wells*, *Incident at
Parga*, *Death in a Distant Land* (winner of the
first *Punch* prize for the best comic crime
novel), *Death in Close-up*, *Mayhem in Parva*,
and *Unwillingly to Vegas*. Nancy Livingston is
married to TV director/producer David Foster
and they live near Ipswich.

Also by Nancy Livingston in
Gollancz Crime

TROUBLE AT AQUITAINE

FATALITY AT BATH & WELLS

INCIDENT AT PARGA

DEATH IN A
DISTANT LAND

by
Nancy Livingston

GOLLANCZ CRIME

Gollancz Crime is an imprint of Victor Gollancz Ltd
14 Henrietta Street, London WC2E 8QJ

First published in Great Britain 1988
by Victor Gollancz Ltd

First Gollancz Crime edition 1991

Copyright © Nancy Livingston 1988

The right of Nancy Livingston to be identified as author of
this work has been asserted by her in accordance with the
Copyright Designs and Patents Act 1988.

A catalogue record for this book
is available from the British Library

ISBN 0 575 05036 5

Printed and bound in Great Britain
by Cox & Wyman Ltd, Reading

*This book is sold subject to the condition that it shall
not, by way of trade or otherwise, be lent, resold,
hired out, or otherwise circulated without the
publisher's prior consent in any form of binding or
cover other than that in which it is published and
without a similar condition including this condition
being imposed on the subsequent purchaser*

For Peggy
in friendship

Chapter One

It was so humid, condensation trickled down the outside of the cool windowpane in rivulets. Inside the hotel room, the whir of the air conditioner was loud, drowning sound from the television. The crowd on the screen, their faces contorted by shouting, could only whisper their excitement. Sweltering in the heat on the far side of the city they were intent on the same purpose as the two in the room, staring at a prison where a man was about to be hanged.

The shot on the screen changed to three small barred windows grouped immediately below the prison roof. Behind the bars, lights were switched on because dusk comes swiftly in Penang. As this happened the crowd gave an involuntary collective gasp.

There was a similar reaction from drinkers watching the same scene in a west London pub. Here it was only midday. There was a trace of summer heat in the pavements outside, enough to vaporize the current downpour. This dampness swept in uninvited as each new customer flung the door wide in his hurry to be out of the wet, and added to the fug. Here, the television was suspended from brackets above the bar; necks were cricked in an effort to see the screen.

"Serve him right." A fat woman feasted her eyes on the three small windows. She shivered deliciously, righteously safe, and tasted the gin in her mouth. "Serve him right, I say," she repeated mechanically. "That'll teach them a lesson."

"I doubt it." An inoffensive-looking man sitting near by couldn't bear to let the statement pass unchallenged. "Killing merely stiffens the resolve of those remaining not to be caught. There's two thousand years of proof if you care to consider the matter." But the barmaid intervened.

"Now then, Mr Pringle," she reproved peaceably. Subjects for aggravation were strictly defined: sex, second-hand cars and salaries. There were never any conclusions but arguments stayed within safe limits. What was on the screen lay outside her guidelines. "I don't know why they're showing us this, do you?"

"Blood lust," he answered sadly. "It increases the ratings whilst impressing ordinary mortals with the power of the State." As if to confirm his words the shot changed to the massed ranks of international news gatherers. Another quick cut and the lens had been refocused on more of the sweaty, expectant faces. "See how well those soft-drink sellers are doing?" he said. "I wonder what they peddled at the crucifixion."

In their luxurious Penang hotel room, the two men waited. They'd never met before today but both were members of the same organization, businessmen, seekers after profit and honoured for it in their respective communities. Secretly, they were two links in a chain that peddled death.

Neither was affected by the death agony inside the small prison cell because it was deserved: their organization had been endangered. A courier had behaved foolishly and been caught; he was paying the inevitable penalty, that was all. Zee, middle-aged and Chinese, listened to the commentary. After a moment or two he translated, his measured, high-pitched sibilance in sharp contrast to the excitement on the screen. "A few minutes more, apparently."

"What are they waiting for?" Ray Vincent was approaching forty, his once athletic physique beginning to blur. Thanks to his share of the profits, he enjoyed an indulgent way of life. That plus a lack of exercise had speeded up the decay. For Zee, his Western smells were offensive, the powerful deodorant, animal lanolin odour from the soap he used—the Chinese ignored them as politely as he could.

"There's been a request for a priest," Zee replied; "the man's a Catholic."

"That won't save him."

"No doubt he believes confession will save his soul."

Ray Vincent ignored the remark and reached for the whisky bottle. Fresh ice clinked inside his glass.

"Another orange juice?"

"No thank you."

"There's nothing he *can* confess to anyway. He spilled everything he knew the night they picked him up, not that it amounted to anything."

Mr Zee bowed in agreement. The organization was thorough. Contact was kept to the minimum: each courier knew the face but not the name of one other person, that was all. Neither Vincent nor Zee knew each other's true identity, only New York had that information.

Each had travelled independently to Penang as a result of a telephone call from New York. Zee waited patiently to be told why he'd been summoned. Vincent must be the executioner since he was not; had there been a reprieve, he knew Vincent would be under orders to kill, for the courier had panicked. He was no use to the organization after that; he had to be eliminated.

And as executioner, Vincent would have the instructions for Zee. The Chinese wondered where in the silky grey and apricot room a weapon had been concealed and whether the Englishman would still be capable of using it? That was the third stiff whisky.

Ray Vincent stared moodily at the screen. It was nine years since he'd last killed a man, nine years and a complete change of life style. He didn't want to remember that other self. He'd almost convinced himself it could be forgotten when the call from New York came, shattering a convenient illusion.

Knowing Zee was watching but careless of what he might report, Vincent drained his glass. He needn't worry any longer, the courier's neck was as good as broken, thanks to the State. And once he'd briefed Zee there was a good chance he could catch tonight's return flight.

"They want you to check out a possible replacement," Vincent said aloud. "He's staying in this hotel; that's why we're here."

"Ah . . ." Mr Zee understood and sucked in air.

"As soon as this farce is over—" Vincent gestured "—we'll take a look at him." On screen, film of the condemned man's parents weeping in their English slum, protesting their son's innocence, filled the delay. "Pa-the-tic." Vincent weighted the syllables impatiently. "He was guilty right enough. The dummy was caught red-handed."

He stopped speaking. The film had disappeared. They were

back live, at the prison, at the three prison windows. The camera zoomed in and isolated the one in the centre. There was no commentary now, nothing but stillness. Ray Vincent didn't move. On the other side of the world, in the London pub, customers were silent. Apart from Mr Pringle reading his *Guardian* everyone stared at the screen.

The silence affected him also for without looking up he asked quietly, "Mavis, d'you think you could switch that thing off?" The barmaid selected another button instead and her customers found themselves watching a snooker match. They looked at one another, outraged: they'd been denied their treat.

In Penang, Ray Vincent asked, "Is that it?" Mr Zee nodded.

"Yes, it's over."

"Good. Come over here."

From behind the curtain they gazed down over the balcony at the swimming pool and the sea beyond; a limpid blue pool separated by white-hot stones from a beach with sluggish grey waves. Around it, an aircrew shrieked and splashed noisily. Unaware of world events, dipping down in and out of continents for a day at a time, their lives spent in a capsule travelling from one swimming pool to the next.

One of the men, a steward, was poised on the springboard. Dark haired, not very tall, slimly built, his eyes were an unexpectedly deep blue against the tanned face. He made very little disturbance as he dived into the pool. As Zee watched, Ray Vincent nodded: "That's him."

"Have you ever considered taking a holiday in Australia?"

"No."

The inoffensive man was proud of that reply, succinct, well-rounded, impossible to misunderstand, but the barmaid shook her head. It was going to be difficult, she might've known. "I've always fancied going," she said firmly, to let him know the matter was as good as settled, "and Ollie Gorman knows a way of getting there cheap."

She'd got his full attention now. In The Bricklayers, Ollie Gorman's offers had, over the years, covered the full spectrum of larceny. "No." Mr Pringle repeated his refusal firmly. Mavis Bignell, however, knew the way not only to his heart but also to his loins.

Beneath the umbrella Mr Pringle groaned silently as her warm flesh nudged against his under his mackintosh. Lately, he'd discovered more than once that he wasn't as young as he thought he was. This evening, Mavis's thigh failed to stimulate him; was it the weather? Alas! Mrs Bignell mistakenly interpreted his sigh as capitulation.

"I'm glad you agree. The air in Australia's like wine, so they say, and you know what a few glasses of that does to you!" She gave a cheerfully lewd wink. "Besides, my friend Mrs Hardie has lost her grandson out there. I said we'd try and find him."

In Penang, the phalanx of news cameras pried out a final glimpse of dead bare feet lolling pigeon-toed over a stretcher and switched off their lights. Officialdom waited uneasily in the mortuary for the grisly ritual to be completed.

"An evangelist!" The man from the embassy whose training had not prevented nausea was grateful for any distraction.

"That's what he said, sir. He told the priest he hadn't thought about it during the trial but tonight he was sure there must be a connection. It was after he'd agreed to be a courier but before he'd actually started working for them; he was chatted up by this Chinese evangelist who claimed to be God's messenger."

"Oh, yes? Where was this?"

"In Singapore. This Chinese bumped into him, apparently quite casually. Offered to buy him a drink then told him details about himself, family stuff, things like that. He also hinted he knew the lad was about to make his first delivery."

"Wasn't he suspicious?"

"That's when the Chinese claimed to be God's messenger and have second sight."

"Good Lord!"

"He referred to the dangers of drug running but the lad pretended he didn't know what the Chinese was talking about. He told the priest he didn't believe he'd ever be caught."

"That's what they all say," the embassy man replied wearily. "It

11

certainly sounds like another member of the gang double-checking. We'll include it in the report . . . have you finished?" The photographer took a final exposure. The mortuary attendant waited in the background, silent and alert, but gleaned nothing further.

In an office behind Macquarie Steet, Kev Macillvenny sat at his desk in a state of slow burn. Enormous hands stretched out in two huge fists of tense muscle. Below, his stomach strained against his trousers, a stomach that followed a continuous ever-increasing curve from his chest to his groin with no indentation between. "Those Pommie bastards!"

Long ago he'd learned to expect to be patronized; it was an integral part of every Pommie's character. Once, oh Glory! God had been on his side when a stupid Whitehall bastard had included a Latin quip in a telex. Not for nothing had Kev Macillvenny attended St Xavier's. He'd sent a forty-line reply entirely in Latin, every sentence ending with a question mark. There'd been absolute silence for weeks after that and he'd never received a reply.

What he couldn't understand was why? Jesuitical teaching hadn't eradicated Kev's essential faith in mankind, his belief as a trained officer of the law that if he and the Brits were on the same side, they should be able to work together.

Why dribble titbits of information when with the whole picture they might take out the gang altogether? What did it matter who got there first, Whitehall or Macquarie Street? Such was Kev Macillvenny's naivety. His fists tightened again in another angry spasm.

Macillvenny's aide Charlie watched the mottled flesh in front of him darken and guessed the cause. He waited for Kev to recover. Sod the Brits. Why worry? There were other ways of finding out what you needed to know.

"There's nothing else come in, you've checked?" As always, Macillvenny was prepared to give the Poms one last chance.

"Nuthin'." Charlie believed in husbanding his resources. Monosyllabic except when under stress, he leaned against a shady bit of wall watching the sun beat down on Kev's bald patch. There was so little hair left you could see the pattern of veins in the skin. Jesus, how long before the silly bugger's blood pressure exploded because of those Poms? Charlie's conscience stirred faintly; he was fond of the old man. "Don't matter, does it, Kev?" he asked, conciliatorily. "We've got hold of the same information."

"That's not the point!" Injured pride replaced Kev's fading anger. "They should've told us. Out of politeness."

"Yeah, well . . ."

"We're both trying to stop the same racket, right?"

"Yes, Kev." The arguments never changed; Charlie was bored.

"So why can't they be frank with us?" There was no answer to that. "What've we got?" Charlie handed him a filched photostat of the embassy man's report. Macillvenny stared morosely at the line: "Previous contact, Chinese evangelist", and the details that followed. "Where would you disappear if you were this bloke and knew you might've been blown?"

"I reckon I might stick around. Singapore's a place any Chinese could hide up in." Kev eyed him thoughtfully.

"You think *they*'d take that much risk? That organization runs a tight ship."

"So where's the risk? We know he'll have a respectable front, some kind of business cover. And he must be a key fella, sent in like that to check the bloke's nerve. So he made a mistake? That bloke's been taken care of but they'll need a replacement—and they'll want *him* given the once-over, too. No, wherever the guy is, he'll lie low for a while, but I reckon he'll be back."

"Any description? Did the bloke give the priest any details?"

"Nah. Guess he'd got other things on his mind."

In a room in Whitehall, Anthony Pelham-Walker gazed out at the rump of the Duke of Wellington's horse. It was his least favourite object. It filled the window frame, but because this room was allocated to holders of Anthony's position, it followed he was stuck with it.

A desk man to the point of constipation. Anthony Pelham-Walker occupied both position and office by reason of attrition. He'd bored his superiors so often over the years they'd promoted him out of self-defence, to rid themselves of his company.

13

Now with a status that meant he lunched alone at his club and with younger, brighter men to do the work of the department, Anthony Pelham-Walker reigned in solitary mandarin splendour. He signed what was put in front of him and incorporated the clever younger men's opinions as his own in finicky memos that were ignored but occupied his days with their composition.

Unfortunately this placid existence had suddenly come under threat. In the dark small hours in his loveless marriage bed Pelham-Walker had been smitten with an awful, undeniable truth, as blinding as that which occurred on the Damascus road: his life, his entire *raison d'être*, was completely meaningless.

For most mandarins, an Alka-Seltzer next morning would've redressed the balance but Anthony Pelham-Walker drank sparingly. On waking, the thought was still there and he knew it wasn't a bad dream. It refused to go away. Like toothache it nagged, occupying his mind to the exclusion of everything else. By late afternoon—he was always the last to leave despite having nothing to do—he was desperate.

It was at that point Crispin Sinclair walked into the room, not so much a clever man as a high-flier determined to reach the top of his grade in as short a time as possible. Which was why he used every opportunity to ingratiate himself. "Oh, you're still here, sir, good . . . A file has been sent over . . . For Information Only, but I thought you ought to see it."

It was the only file that had arrived on his desk that day and Anthony Pelham-Walker seized it with trembling hands. Was there still some small task, some justification for the gong that in the fullness of time would undoubtedly be his? He pored over the sheet it contained, running his finger along the words.

Dear God, thought Crispin, I thought even in Cambridge they learned to read. Batman suddenly looked up, his eyes shining, and Crispin felt distinctly uneasy. "A nugget of information, Sinclair!"

"A—minuscule—nugget, sir?" Crispin replied tentatively; and none of our business anyway, he thought. He'd only brought it in to make the stupid bugger feel important. "I'm afraid, at this stage, we cannot put it higher than that," he added judiciously.

"Has it been acted upon?" Good Grief!

"Not in so many words, sir . . . it's been fed into the computer, analysed and so forth but acted upon—no." Sinclair forced himself to give a confidential smile. "I fear, even in our department, we consider there's very little more that can be achieved—at this stage." And he certainly wasn't going to screw things up by offering inane suggestions to Scotland Yard, he'd got his career to think of. "One cannot see any possible way in which anyone could—act—at present?" Pelham-Walker nodded agreement. Crispin swallowed with relief. For a moment he thought Batman had lost the rest of his marbles.

"So what happens next?" asked Pelham-Walker, his shoulders beginning to droop.

"We wait, sir. We'll be told, naturally, if this particular oriental gentleman crops up anywhere else." He gave a gay, confident laugh. "We haven't bothered the Australians with it because, frankly, we don't consider it all that important."

"Oh, I quite agree. As you say, we must wait and see. But keep me informed." Pelham-Walker handed back the file a mite reluctantly, Crispin considered. As he left the office he glanced at his watch. Good Lord, he'd nearly made himself late!

Chapter Two

In matters of the heart, Mavis Bignell had until the advent of Mr
Pringle been a gallant loser. But after their first encounter when
she, naked and deputizing for the usual model, faced Beginners in
Oils, Mavis realized that at last Fate had taken a hand.

For one so well endowed by nature the years of waiting had been
a trial. Of course there were always those ready for "a bit of a
nibble" but they got short shrift. Mavis came from a background
where "saving oneself" was ingrained. Herbert Bignell had been a
terrible disappointment but she didn't seek consolation elsewhere.
As well as pride in her reputation, Mavis was also convinced that
someday "Mr Right" would come along.

When on that fateful evening Mr Pringle had been so overcome,
so overwhelmed by the mass of sculpted pearly-pink flesh and the
Titian triangle, Mavis's sense of values underwent a sea-change.
She watched the quiet, inoffensive stranger attack his canvas with
demonic energy. She'd never met an artist before but no doubt
about it: this was it, this was Real Life! His picture, a remarkably
thick composition, was finished in three hours flat; they carried it
between them up to Mrs Bignell's bedroom where, as she modestly
described events afterwards, Mr Pringle had swept her off her feet.

If they'd been drawn together out of loneliness—for Mr
Pringle's beloved Renée had died not long before the late,
unlamented Herbert—romance quickly replaced it. Once or twice
Mr Pringle suggested matrimony but Mavis declared she preferred
the status quo. "In my experience, marriage can kill love stone-
dead. People get careless about hurting one another's feelings. I
couldn't bear that to happen to us."

All the same, she had to admit these days life was a little dreary.
The sparkle had disappeared from their relationship. It seemed to
her as if Mr Pringle had withdrawn into a melancholy world of his

own and being of a naturally cheery disposition herself, Mrs Bignell found it dispiriting. When she heard Ollie Gorman offering his cut-price tickets to Australia the same day she herself had had an enormous unexpected stroke of luck, she knew it must be "a sign"; she and Mr Pringle would shake the dust off their feet and enjoy themselves.

It had taken longer than she'd anticipated; Mr P had held out against all manner of persuasion. Tonight she'd wheedled him to accompany her to Mrs Hardie's, ostensibly to comfort her friend over the missing grandchild. What Mavis had omitted to mention was that she'd invited Ollie Gorman too, and this was weighing on her conscience.

As they stepped over the threshold, Mr Pringle shrank from the overhearty greeting. "Come on in, squire, don't be shy. We're all friends in here." Ollie's florid red face dwarfed the tiny kitchen. Half-hidden, the neat small shape of Mrs Hardie bobbed out round the side of him.

"It is kind of you to come round—" she began.

"Of course it is, but what did you expect?" Ollie Gorman demanded. "At The Bricklayers, we know Mr Pringle. If he says he'll come, then he will, he's not the sort to let you down. He's Mavie's friend, after all." Ollie leered.

"Now just one moment . . ." Mr Pringle was shocked; had he been inveigled here on a false premise? "If you and Mrs Bignell wish to discuss her travel arrangements, I must point out she will be flying to Australia alone. I shall not be accompanying her, I simply cannot afford to." Mavis's departure was an established fact and the date chalked up above the bar. The darts final between The Bricklayers and The White Hart had been postponed in consequence.

"You haven't agreed—yet—" Ollie Gorman smirked with elephantine subtlety "—because you haven't let me tell you how inexpensive it is. Shall I tell him now, Mavie? Is your friend ready for the shock of a lifetime or should we steady his nerves first?"

Mrs Hardie recognized the prompt and hastened in with her line. "Would you like a drink, Mr Pringle? From a bottle of sherry? Mr Gorman was kind enough to bring one."

"Ollie, dear, not Mister. Like I said, we're all friends here."

"I'm afraid I haven't got proper glasses."

"Would you like me to pour?" Mavis asked.

"Oh, would you!" The flustered hostess hid behind Ollie again. "I'm afraid I'm not used to doing it."

"Tell Mr Pringle about Ben," Mavis suggested tactfully. Mrs Hardie glanced automatically at the photographs on the mantel-piece.

"It's over six months since I heard from him. Gary took him to Australia without telling Linda—just collected Ben from outside the school one day. I was away visiting friends at the time. Of course Gary and Linda had split up by then."

Mavis handed Mr Pringle his sherry. "Gary always wanted to go back to Australia but Linda refused to go with him."

"That wasn't the only thing they argued about." Mrs Hardie was candid in her betrayal of her daughter. "He and Linda used to have hundreds of rows. I don't know how Gary put up with it as long as he did."

"What I can't quite understand—" Mr Pringle was less polite than usual. He preferred dry Spanish sherry and what Ollie Gorman had supplied was a sickly, dark brown substance "—is why his mother—Linda, isn't it?—hasn't tried to secure the boy's return through the proper channels."

"It costs too much." Mrs Hardie sighed. "She did go to a solicitor. She made an appointment but when she come home she told me it wasn't any use. They'd got joint custody, too, you see." She sighed again. "It didn't do me no good either. I've been stuck with her ever since Gary went. She moved back just when I was all set to go to one of them warden places. I'd got my name down and there was a vacancy."

"As regards Ben—" Mr Pringle clung to the point "—surely your daughter should be the one to go and search for him?"

"I told you," Mrs Hardie repeated patiently, "we can't afford it, either of us."

"Show Mr Pringle that last postcard you had," Mavis suggested. It was produced from a worn handbag.

"You can read it if you like," Mrs Hardie told him.

It was a view of a small Australian town. The roads were wide, the buildings bright, clean and single-storey. Across the plate-glass window of an ice-cream parlour on one corner of the crossroads someone had scribbled an arrow in biro.

"'Dear Gran,'" Mr Pringle read on the back, "'We are in Bathurst eating banana splits. Dad and me come here this morning from Sydney. Love, Ben. XXX'"

"Gary's a truck driver. He wrote when he first went saying he'd send for Linda and me as soon as he and Ben got fixed up somewhere," Mrs Hardie told them sadly, "but we never heard from him again. In that letter Gary said the Australian sunshine would do Ben good." The grandmother was near to tears. "I hope it has . . . I thought I could trust Gary."

"I'm very sorry," Mr Pringle said helplessly. In the small room, the emotion was disturbing. "If there was any way I could help . . . but I simply cannot afford to accompany Mrs Bignell to Australia, much as I wish to do so." Ollie Gorman looked as though he was about to spring to life but Mavis frowned; nevertheless, the time had come for her to confess.

"You could afford it if you let me treat you."

"That's impossible." Mr Pringle was embarrassed that she should say such a thing in front of strangers. Besides, as a retired member of Her Majesty's Inland Revenue he was extremely conscious of the rules concerning gifts.

"I didn't tell you before—I cashed in my Premium Bonds and put them on the Derby," Mavis said quietly. "They hadn't done anything for years, it seemed a waste leaving them where they were."

"I tried to give her a tip but it was a good job she didn't listen," Ollie announced. "Mavie was right and I was wrong—and she put it all on the nose, she's a goer all right."

Despite his aversion Mr Pringle had to ask: "What happened?"

"It won, sixteen to one. I made just over two thousand pounds, two thousand and forty eight to be exact." Years of mental arithmetic enabled him to work the sum out backwards.

"Good grief! You put all that on a horse!"

"I was very careful which one I chose." Mavis was huffy. "I didn't pick any old horse—this one had nice eyes. I didn't tell you at the time because I knew what you'd say."

Two thousand pounds! "You should invest it in life insurance,"

Mr Pringle murmured faintly, "and include the interest in your next tax return—"

"Blow that for a laugh," his lover replied vigorously. "I've always wanted to visit Australia and I want you to come with me. There's no fun going on your own."

"And when you hear how little it'll cost you—" Ollie couldn't restrain himself any longer, his bracelet clanked against his watch as he seized Mr Pringle's arm "—you'll wonder why you never considered going there before."

Chapter Three

It was one of those pairs of small brick-built cottages that crop up unexpectedly among the dunes and industrial hinterland on the far side of Heathrow. Long ago they'd been homes to families who scraped a living from these gravel pits and marshes; now they were bought by those who needed a base close to the airport.

The dark-haired steward, Evan Jones, lay on his divan bed, smoking duty-free cigarettes. He wore an old vest and jeans. The room was bare of furniture apart from the bed, one chair and some packing cases. The area round his bed was neat; clean clothes were folded in their temporary storage boxes, ash from his cigarette was tipped meticulously into the container in his hand, and the coverlet on which he lay was tucked in at the corners with precision.

The rest of the room was strewn with debris, tools, decorating equipment and tiles, laboriously imported box by heavy box after trips to Rome. Piled in a heap in one corner were souvenirs, ready to adorn the half-finished Spanish-style bar.

Upstairs the two bedrooms were completely bare. In the bathroom the towels were from hotels where he'd stayed. Ashtrays had international names. Nowhere was there the stamp of Evan himself: the cottage was a rag-bag of junk, collected by a scavenger who'd flown round the world and seen nothing of it except hotel rooms, bars and swimming pools.

The steward had been stripping wallpaper when the second phone call came. He'd made no effort to continue, fear had paralyzed him. The hand holding the cigarette still trembled. Despite his instinctive tidiness, some of the ash spilled on to the floor. Above, wide-bodied jets made the ground vibrate, and less than a mile away motorway traffic kept up a constant roar. He wasn't aware of any of it. Evan Jones was far too terrified: he was trapped.

Yesterday when the first, expected message came, he'd asked the anonymous voice to relay one back for him. He'd worked it out very carefully indeed, written it down. Even so his voice shook as he read out the words. The caller hadn't spoken, he'd hung up. That was when Evan realized his hands were wet with sweat.

He tried to convince himself it was going to be all right; the silence proved it. Whoever *they* were, they'd accepted his assurances and were prepared to release him from bondage. He'd even managed a few hours' sleep after he'd drunk enough whisky.

Today the telephone mocked him. The latest in crazy technology, a scarlet plastic shape with a gold cord, it was designed to be an amusing accessory on the Spanish bar. When he'd answered it an hour ago, the tinny voice had destroyed his peace of mind for ever. That red toy was no longer a phone but a bomb that had blown his life apart. There would be no more sleep.

Confirmation of the threats the caller had made arrived in the post: photographs. Evan Jones stared at them again, horribly fascinated by the irrefutable evidence they contained.

It was a sequence of three pictures. The first, slightly fuzzy, had been taken in a hotel room moments after he'd lifted the first consignment from its hiding place. Too late, Evan remembered the sudden unexpected arrival of a chambermaid coming in with a laden trolley. The second, snatched from a car that must've been following him, showed Evan making a prearranged drop in Sydney. The last, inside a Hong Kong nightclub, was much clearer; he'd been facing the concealed camera that time, a stupid happy smile on his face as he accepted the wad of notes.

Evan sobbed aloud, cursing himself for being a fool. When *they* first approached him, he'd been wildly excited as well as indignant. His immediate reaction had been to report what had happened, but after an hour or two he began to consider the matter. Supposing he only did a couple of trips, then refused? The money would certainly be handy—how could *they* force him to go on?

He would keep his side of the bargain, he'd given them his word; he'd never tell a soul. Nor would there be anything to incriminate their organization—the irony of that finally hit Evan. The stranger who'd first spoken to him in Penang was quite right when he'd said there would be no way he could identify them. Every contact had been by phone. Evan had only met one other person but he didn't know his real name. It was safer that way, the man claimed.

Three trips, that's all Evan had decided; three, maybe four, then he'd chuck it in. He congratulated himself on his strength of will. There could only be a minimal risk in three trips.

To date, it had been seven. Evan needed the money because he'd been taken off the profitable transatlantic run with its dollar expenses and sent east instead, where allowances were much smaller and currencies unstable. The rate of exchange against the rupee was ludicrous, you couldn't pay the gas bill with those.

Lying on the divan, he found himself thinking of his family in Wales. Fourteen of them and he the only one with a job. My God, how proud they'd been when the airline took him on, treating him like some bloody hero. And then when he told them he'd bought a house . . . Oh hell! They wouldn't be cheering when they got to hear about this!

He flung the photos aside. He'd promised Mam she could come here for a holiday, too. He wanted to prove that he'd arrived. To show her their family could feel proud. What a joke! Evan looked about. He'd have to do the place up quickly and sell it. He'd even have to give up his precious job and disappear, lose his identity, if he wanted to be truly safe. Maybe he'd never escape them, ever!

Suddenly he was on his feet. Fear had gone. Instead, he was very, very angry. There must be a way out. All those months without work—was he going to give up without a fight? Stop being so bloody feeble-minded! Forget about being caught, just bloody well think of a plan!

Evan plugged in the kettle—coffee would settle his stomach if his hands stopped shaking long enough to make it—and unfolded a large sheet of paper. Thin black lines criss-crossed in a dense geometric pattern. Down one side were flight numbers and across the top, days of the week. It was the company's eastern flight schedule for the next three months.

Evan picked up his duty roster and out of habit checked his next departure and flight details one more time. Tomorrow, Monday 31st, leaving Heathrow on Flight 974 at 1000 hours GMT. Wait a tick . . . Evan ran his finger down the thin line, across, and down again. A night-stop at Abu Dhabi; but the flight out of there the following morning had an asterisk—it was a charter! Christ, there might just be a way out after all. *They* had assumed he would be on a routine ten-day Sydney terminator but he would be outside the regular route pattern once he picked up that charter!

For the first time since the tinny voice destroyed his peace of mind Evan Jones began to breathe easily. This might be his only chance, he must use it carefully. If he loused it up this time, he could be a goner.

It had taken several weeks for Ollie Gorman to come up with a pair of tickets, after all. Their date of departure had been put back three times. It all depended, Ollie explained, on there being spare seats on charters, but Mr Pringle didn't believe it. He fully expected to be turned back at Heathrow or, worse still, have to pay extra before the airline would accept them. He made the mistake of confiding his gloom to Mrs Bignell and she reacted extremely sharply.

They had gone round for a final visit to Mrs Hardie, to collect one or two photographs of Ben and a letter to give to her young grandson in the unlikely event that they find him. Mr Pringle was very doubtful but Mavis continued optimistic. "You never know" was her constant refrain.

Mrs Hardie, neat in her sensible trouser suit, perched birdlike on a corner of her kitchen table and poured them tea. Gone was the shy awkwardness of their first encounter. On her own, mistress of her kitchen, she chatted happily. "Isn't it exciting, you're off at last! And it's ever so kind of you to take the trouble. I'm ever so grateful."

"I'm afraid we can't promise—" Mr Pringle began but Mavis interrupted.

"You haven't heard anything, I suppose? Since we were here last?" Mrs Hardie shook her head and gave a fierce sniff. "Never mind, dear. Is this the latest photo you have of Ben?" Tears were swiftly, unobtrusively wiped away.

"Yes. Taken at school last year, that's why he's in uniform."

Mr Pringle sipped his tea. There were more family photos on the walls. One was of Ben when he'd obviously taken a tumble and had a hefty plaster cast on one leg. Others, from the nineteen-fifties as far as Mr Pringle could judge from the length of the shorts, showed a much older youth with the same startling blue whites to his eyes. The family resemblance between the two was strong.

"That's Ben's uncle." Mrs Hardie spoke softly and her voice trembled a little. "Linda's brother. He'd have been thirty-seven next birthday . . ."

"I'm sorry." The implication was obvious. "Was it—an accident?" Mrs Hardie sighed.

"Not really. We'd been expecting it but it still came as a shock." In the silence Mr Pringle looked again at the dead youth then at the picture in Mrs Bignell's hand.

"They're extremely alike."

"Yes." Mrs Hardie's voice sounded flat as if the possible loss of her grandson as well as her son was too much to bear. Mr Pringle wondered uneasily if he could speed their departure. He'd no intention of raising false hopes in Mrs Hardie concerning Ben. He tried to signal to Mrs Bignell but she had their brochure in her hand.

"Would you like to see our itinerary, dear? It should be the holiday of a lifetime." Mr Pringle's heart sank; from experience he knew this could take a very long time indeed. Ever since he'd capitulated and agreed to be treated, Mavis's ideas had continued to expand. It usually began with a phrase he'd learned to dread: "As we're going all that way, it seems silly not to . . ."

Since their first visit here when he'd finally given in, their holiday had expanded from just over two weeks to six. He had to admit it was possible to see a great deal of Australia comparatively cheaply and how silly it was to go all that way and not see as much as possible, but he was beginning to wonder whether he would survive the trip.

Under pressure, Ollie Gorman had admitted he'd no idea who their fellow travellers would be. Scientists of some sort, he thought, travelling to Australia via Bangkok.

"We stay in Thailand for a couple of days, then we go by train all the way down through Malaysia to Singapore." Mrs Bignell's eyes were warm as she conjured up the picture. "Ever so romantic. Past all those rubber plantations Somerset Maugham used to write about."

25

"Oh, yes?" Mrs Hardie's books came from a different shelf in the library.

"Then we pick up a flight at Singapore for Sydney—I'm really looking forward to that. We go with these scientific people all the way up Australia. You know how they have Greyhound buses in America? Well down there they call them Wallabies."

"I always get sick on a coach," said Mrs Hardie. "What happens at night? D'you stay in hotels?"

"We camp out under the stars."

"Camp!" Mrs Hardie couldn't believe it. "You ever done any, Mavis?"

"I shall be all right." Mrs Bignell was adamant. "Mr Pringle once put up a tent during the war, didn't you dear?"

"The brochure assures us that the tents 'are simplicity itself, and help is available should it be required'," he protested, but Mrs Hardie shook her head.

"I don't like the sound of that. Those brochures are full of lies. You read it in the papers every day. I hope you'll be comfortable. I wouldn't fancy it. Have another cup of tea before you go?"

"According to our itinerary, on one of the days we stop for lunch in the town where Ben sent his postcard. Bathurst."

"Do you?" Mrs Hardie was attentive.

"Yes, and I thought we'd go to that ice-cream place—" Mavis broke off because someone had entered the kitchen.

"Oh, there you are Linda." Mrs Hardie didn't seem particularly pleased to see her daughter. "This is Mr Pringle who's going to look for Ben."

The woman who came into the room took Mr Pringle by surprise. She was tall and fleshy with a mass of blonde hair and without the spare delicate build of her mother, nor the distinctive blue eyes of her dead brother. As Linda greeted each of them in turn, Mr Pringle had the feeling she was making an effort to subdue her personality. He could imagine her enjoying a knees-up at The Bricklayers much more easily than living in this finicky neat kitchen full of knick-knacks.

"How do you do? We will do our best to find your boy although I fear that cannot be much. Australia is such a very large country

". . ." Mr Pringle was embarrassed. Mrs Bignell, as usual, was overconfident.

"Don't you worry, Linda. If anyone can find him, Mr Pringle can. We're going to Bathurst and we'll ask in the ice-cream parlour. If I show them Ben's photo, someone might remember."

Linda glanced at it briefly. "Yes, they might." She sounded as unconvinced as Mr Pringle. He felt inward relief; unlike Mrs Hardie, Linda obviously realized their chances were slim.

"I wish I thought it likely . . ." he began and she looked at him in understanding.

"Don't worry . . . You'll do what you can, I expect."

Mrs Hardie's small shoulder blades hunched against any suggestion of defeat. "You will try," she pleaded.

Mrs Bignell stood up, cramming photographs, letter and brochure into her handbag. "You leave it to us," she replied. "Australia may be a big place but there aren't many people in it, it said so in *Reader's Digest*."

The paragraph was on the front page. Headed "Drug traffic hits new high!" what followed was a vitriolic attack on the attempts of New South Wales's authorities to stem the flow. Charlie read it on the ferry over from Manly. Looked like Kev's blood pressure was in for another bad day.

Chapter Four

"This aeroplane's got an upstairs."

"Mmmm . . ." Mr Pringle didn't care, he still felt ill. The effort of following five thousand other people the eight miles to a departure gate, then climbing into this Odeon cinema, of being herded to a seat that squashed the coins in his pockets into the flesh of his buttocks, had defeated him. He was hemmed in by strangers, he couldn't move—he couldn't breathe! Half a mile away, someone was waving an oxygen mask. Mr Pringle was desperate for air. Never before had he experienced such claustrophobia—and how could an Odeon transport this mass of bodies half-way round the world? It was ridiculous!

Mavis had solved the problem of her seat; she'd refused it. "Look, dear, these are for anorexics," she said cheerfully. "Where's the one I've booked?" The stewardess had been in the job too long.

"The width of an economy seat was laid down in the Warsaw Convention of 1948, madam."

"We were all thinner in 1948," Mavis told her coldly, "we still had ration books." She was magnificently arrayed in fuchsia and stood her ground. She pointed to the distant front cabin. "What about one of those? They look much wider." The stewardess was outraged.

"Madam, that is the First Class!"

The line of those waiting to be seated now snaked back as far as the tarmac. The purser made frantic hand-signals. Despite her fury the stewardess had to give in. "As a temporary measure, may I suggest that you sit in the lounge for take-off?" Mrs Bignell smiled, satisfied. She turned to Mr Pringle.

"See you later, dear, when I find where they've hidden the bar."

Alone, he stared out through yellowing cracked Perspex in the porthole and tried to forget everything he'd ever read about pressurization failure. At a rough guess, there were fifty-eight rows of elderly cripples between him and the emergency exit, so why worry? He couldn't escape.

Music was available to soothe his fears but even as he reached for the headphones, a voice from the Tannoy informed those on the port side that their speakers were no longer working. Mr Pringle wondered gloomily if they'd had any similar problems with the engines?

"You go up this spiral staircase and you come out on the first floor," Mavis continued.

By some miracle they'd become airborne after all and had stayed aloft long enough for the first meal to be flung at them. The inevitable queues formed outside the lavatories. So much for emergency procedures—Mr Pringle could no longer even see the fire exits because of the anxious throng. Mrs Bignell, flushed and happy, fought her way through to where he sat in the rear cabin.

"It's nicer upstairs, less crowded," she reported.

"Any bedrooms?" His internal organs had been dangerously compressed for too long. "A bunk would do."

"There's only this place they call the lounge. Very shabby. The plastic's peeling off the walls and the stuffing's come out. You can see right through to the metal. The captain's sitting up there. Claims he's got an upset tummy." Mr Pringle was immediately awake.

"Who's flying this blessed thing then?"

"Colin."

"Who the hell's Colin?"

"Ssh!" Mavis never failed to be shocked by language. "He's the first officer. I've been chatting to him while he had his supper. Steak and kidney. He said he was glad of a bit of company. He showed me how some of the little levers worked—"

"What!"

"Keep your voice down. It's perfectly safe to sit in the cockpit provided you don't pull any of the knobs. *Colin* says the skipper's shamming. He says he's in a sulk because he's been passed over for promotion." Mr Pringle closed his eyes. "Mind you, it's Colin I feel sorry for." Mavis was solemn. "D'you know, his wife's two-timing him with a British Caledonian first officer. Every time Colin takes off from Heathrow, the other one's winging in from Gatwick—isn't it a shame? He was nearly crying when he told me about it."

So was Mr Pringle. This dilapidated two-storey cinema, hurtling through space in sole charge of an emotional cuckold . . . "How can one man eat supper, fly the thing and keep a lookout?"

"Oh, they don't bother looking. Colin says the speed these things travel, you wouldn't even see the one you hit. Well, ta-ta dear. We'll be in Abu Dhabi soon, that's where the crews change over." She bent lower and murmured, "If the next steward's friendly, maybe he'll let me stay in the upstairs lounge."

They disembarked into a hot dry night and straggled across to an artificial air-cooled oasis. Mr Pringle gazed down from under a vast mosaic palm tree at fellow travellers round the fountain below. Mrs Bignell had disappeared to strip off some of her clothes. "I plan to peel off the layers as we go," she'd told him. The thought helped distract him from the terror of flying.

From his vantage point, it looked as though others should be encouraged to follow her example. Some passengers were still in suits and ties. One carried a mac and another, inexplicably, an umbrella. It was so British it was embarrassing.

"There we are . . . that's better." Her jacket was gone but the silky pink skirt remained, topped by a sleeveless, low-necked flowery blouse. Mavis now sported exotic earrings and a scarf wrapped turban-style round the vivid hair.

"I say!" said Mr Pringle and Mavis puffed out her magnificent chest.

"I'm glad you like it. I think I'll go back to the aeroplane, dear. See if I can find the new crew. Would you like to join me if there's another spare seat in the lounge?" He shook his head.

"No thank you. If possible, I shall try and sleep on the next leg."

There was an armed Arab guard barring the exit back to the aircraft. Mr Pringle watched Mavis approach, saw the man's glance descend to her chest . . . and remain there, transfixed. If Mavis's figure was more suited to a bygone era in the West, here at least it was appreciated.

They chatted; the man laughed and stood aside to let her pass.

*

Evan Jones had worked out his plan very carefully indeed. He went through it again as he set out champagne glasses for the first-class customers. It all depended on one as yet unknown factor.

A passenger had come back early, he could hear her climbing the stairs. Like an overblown peony she stood before him, smiling plumply. "Hallo, dear, I'm Mavis. Shall I give you a hand? I'm used to bar work and I can't stand the thought of being idle all the way to Thailand." It was fate, thought Evan.

Mr Pringle tried to sleep. He ignored the offer of duty-free cigarettes, the second dinner and the four-gallon jug of boiling coffee that hovered dangerously close to his ear. The lights were lowered and gangsters began shouting at one another on the screen (noiselessly for those on the port side). He closed his eyes. Someone touched his arm. A steward in a tuxedo leaned over to pass him a glass. "From Mavis." The young man's eyes were very blue against the tanned skin. "One of her margaritas . . . She's the life and soul of a party going on in the first-class lounge—want to come?" He'd got an engaging grin. Mr Pringle smiled in response.

"Thank you, but no. Please tell Mrs Bignell I'm glad she's enjoying herself." The steward laughed.

"She's doing that all right—the other passengers are loving it. She's teaching some Americans to sing 'Roll Out the Barrel'."

On her way to freshen up as dawn flooded the cabin, Mrs Bignell paused by his seat. She looked bright-eyed and happy. "Hasn't it been a lovely flight? Did you manage to sleep?" Loyally and because she'd treated him to the ticket, Mr Pringle lied and said that he had. "I've found out about the people we're travelling with, these scientists going to Australia."

"Oh, yes?"

"There's forty of them but this was the only aircraft they could charter. That's why there were spare seats for blokes like Ollie to sell."

He was astonished. "Sounds very high-powered. What exactly do they do?"

"They're phonies."

31

"Pardon?"

"That's what it says on the labels, FONEs. I presume that's how you say it. It stands for 'Friends of Nuclear Energy'."

"Then why are they going to Australia? Surely they don't have nuclear energy down there?"

"That's what I thought. Rum, isn't it."

After joining the queue for a wash, she had more to impart. "It's highly secret. To do with the government. One of the wives told me."

"If it's a secret . . . ?"

"She's had a tiff with her hubby. She says she doesn't care any more who knows about it. You see, when they left for the airport this morning he managed to reverse the Volvo over their pet rabbit. She said the only memory she'll carry round Australia is of her children, screaming over this nasty mess lying in the road—"

"Yes, yes." He'd been looking forward to breakfast. "So what sort of secret mission is it?"

"Well . . ." Mavis squeezed in beside him to keep it confidential. "You know how people tried to stop firms burying nuclear waste at home—got up petitions, that sort of thing—then it was election time and the government decided none of the sites were really suitable because they'd all got voters living in them?"

"Yes?"

"Then they wanted to bury it under the Irish Sea but people were worried about what it might do to the fish?"

Mr Pringle nodded: "Understandably so."

"Well that's what this is all about. These scientists are visiting Australia, hoping to find a suitable place to dump the waste down there."

"You're joking!"

"No, I'm not. As part of the bicentennial celebration of the founding of Australia, the lady said."

"Good grief!"

"Her husband's told her if they do find somewhere suitable, he might be given the Queen's Award to Industry."

Bangkok was heavy with a torpid heat that sapped Mr Pringle's strength. He was thankful all he had to do was struggle on to an

32

air-conditioned bus. His fellow travellers, still in their suits, looked even worse than he did. Mrs Bignell settled beside him. "The crew are staying at the same hotel, isn't that nice? I've invited Evan to join us when we go sightseeing tomorrow."

He remembered the lilt in the voice. "Is Evan the steward?"

"He's a lovely boy." She watched as the last of their party climbed into the coach. "What a miserable looking bunch of sods these scientists are. Fancy sending them on a good-will mission."

"Is that what it's supposed to be?" Mr Pringle hoped the Australians would understand.

The road into the city was a highway, raised up, with traffic streaming past on either side: Thai people on scooters or driving small battered lorries, who smiled and raised their hands in greeting. Conditioned by years of sullen London faces Mr Pringle lifted his timidly in reply. They passed hoardings covered in exotic curved script—he couldn't understand a word. At every street corner, in front of skyscraper offices, were tiny shrines decked with flowers where devout passers-by knelt to pray.

He was in the abroad, no doubt about it, in the mysterious, beguiling East, the downfall of so many foreigners. He squeezed Mrs Bignell's hand. "Isn't it marvellous? We've actually got here!"

She saw the gleam in his eye. After her all-night partying, Mavis was tired. My word, she thought, I hope I can manage to keep up. "What we both need first," she said firmly, "is a kip."

The hotel was a vast dark cavern with heavy wooden ceilings. Everywhere, a mass of tourists eddied: Germans, Dutch, and, it seemed, thousands of Japanese. He and Mavis were stranded in a sea of people, anchored to their suitcases.

"Hi, you two OK?"

"Oh, Evan—can you sort out which is our room?" The steward nodded at Mavis, made his way confidently to the reception desk and returned with a couple of forms.

"Fill these in and give me your passports." He grinned at Mr Pringle's expression. "It's perfectly safe, honest. Everyone has to hand them in out here."

"I see."

"Look," he said, returning with their key, "I'm sure you're

bushed right now but when you want to go and eat, there's a marvellous place just across the road—let me show you." As they walked back into the blinding sunshine, Mr Pringle suggested hesitantly that he might like to join them. The young man shook his head.

"Not tonight, thanks. You go and enjoy yourselves. We'll meet up tomorrow, after breakfast, and 'do' the town. 'Bye."

"Isn't he nice." Mavis watched him go. "Who says all young people are yobs nowadays—Evan's such a polite boy." They began to walk towards the lifts. Mr Pringle's thoughts had already reached the seventh floor.

"I wonder if our room will have a double bed?"

Chapter Five

The day had satiated them. It had begun easily enough, on the river. They had sailed to where a canal branched off and old women in boats, protected from the blistering heat by vast coolie hats, hawked vegetables and watermelons. Mavis was entranced. Today, abandoning pink for shades of caramel and orange and framed by her sunshade, she was, Mr Pringle thought happily, his own exquisite tropical bloom.

All the commerce of the city had been on that river. Young bloods whizzed past in "hot rods", the vast engines anchored to their flimsy boats by nothing more than shafts. The wash from huge barges lumbering up and down rocked their motor launch. Everywhere there were contrasts: Western-style hotels facing wooden houses across the Chao Phya, concrete buildings interspersed with the delicate shapes of pagodas.

In the afternoon, the pace quickened. They were dazzled by porcelain palaces studded with jewels, temples roofed in marble, by innumerable statues covered in gold, guarded by strange mythical beasts and crowned by the omnipresent Garuda bird.

Finally, in a temple containing a reclining Buddha nearly fifty metres long, Mrs Bignell threw in the sponge. "I'm sorry, dears, I can't manage another step, my feet are so swollen." She lifted one daintily for them to inspect. "I'll never get my shoes back on as it is."

In the taxi, she and Mr Pringle promised themselves they'd come back tomorrow, commiserating with Evan who had to fly home to England instead. That evening the three of them sat in an open-air restaurant amid Greek columns, soothed by fountains choreographed to Beethoven, Bizet and the Beatles. It was kitsch, it was delightful. Mavis paused in the midst of her satay to demand: "Isn't this—magic!" and Mr Pringle readily agreed. He raised a solemn glass.

"To the swift quadruped with compelling eyes."

"What I still can't get over—" Evan returned to an earlier theme "—is those blokes renovating the statues today, surrounded by gold leaf and jewels. Each box must've been worth a fortune—what's to stop any of them pinching the lot?" Mr Pringle felt a slight irritation that Evan should ruffle their mood. He quoted their guide's response to the same question: " 'Who would want to rob the Lord Buddha?' " But Evan scoffed: "Almost everyone I know . . . and talking of Buddhas, what about that other one made of solid gold? How big would you say it was—fourteen, fifteen feet?"

"Something like that." Mr Pringle wanted to relax and listen to the music. "I don't think I've ever seen a more serene face." Evan stared at him.

"Serene! Imagine what you'd get for it? I didn't see any security, did you? Fancy keeping a king's ransom in some shabby old temple in a back alley!" Mr Pringle sighed.

"They have a different set of values here. I'm shamefully ignorant, I admit, but their religion obviously brings tranquillity rather than greed. Perhaps theirs is a better way?" Evan's eyes were suddenly hard.

"You know something? All that'll disappear the minute someone works out it's worth his while to nick the thing, bet you anything you like." Mr Pringle wasn't a gambling man and such an attitude disturbed him.

"I'm sad to hear you say so."

"Well, I like it here." Mavis pushed away her empty plate. "I like the people, the place—the food's smashing. It's been a lovely day so don't let's spoil it." Evan twirled the stem of his glass.

"It's OK for some . . . I know too much about poverty." Mr Pringle thought it prudent not to hear.

"I do wish you'd let me take your photo, Evan," Mavis protested. "I wanted to show them at The Bricklayers: 'Look what I managed to pick up—and he never even asked for a tip!' "

"No way." Evan was sunny again. "By the time you two get back you'll have forgotten about me. Holidays are like that. Hope the ones I took of you come out all right, though."

"Give me your address anyway." Mrs Bignell scrabbled in her bag for a pen. "I want to send you a postcard when we get to Australia." Mr Pringle listened indulgently. He agreed with Evan, theirs was an ephemeral acquaintanceship, then he chided himself; he hadn't allowed for Mavis's kind heart. She wouldn't forget the boy.

The steward dictated an address in Carmarthen. "I've got a place near the airport," he explained, "but I haven't been there long. The postman sometimes forgets I live there, so I send most of my mail home to Mam. She looks after it."

"I won't send a rude one then." Mavis winked. "Not if your Ma's going to read it first." Evan picked up Ben's photo from among the debris on the table.

"This the kid you're hoping to find? What amazing eyes. Looks a bit skinny, though."

"Poor little mite," Mavis agreed. "Always in and out of hospital, the accidents he's had. Let's hope Australia has done him some good after all. Now what was your aunty's address in Sydney?" Mr Pringle groaned, silently. Not more vanished relatives! She must've caught his mood because she said quickly, "Evan was expecting to go to Australia. He didn't realize he'd only get as far as Bangkok because of the charter."

"It's aunty's birthday." The steward was apologetic. "If you could send the parcel for me, that's all. It'll be too late by the time I get to England—and I promised Mam. Here—" He pulled out a five-pound note "—this is to cover the postage—I insist," for Mr Pringle was beginning to murmur a protest. "Take a taxi from the hotel to the post office, there should be sufficient. I've already addressed it—it's just a few books, if Customs want to know," he added, "some paperbacks aunty can't buy in Australia." Then to Mavis, "Thanks again for helping me out."

"That's all right, dear, thank *you* for a lovely day!" Wine and exercise had left Mrs Bignell feeling mellow.

"Well—" Evan looked at his watch "—if I'm to make that five a.m. call . . ." He rose and stretched out his hand, "Thank you again." Mr Pringle shook it politely, mindful that it was the steward who had found them a guide and organized the day. He must stop feeling jealous of the young, it was the worst sin the old

37

could commit. He watched with scarcely a qualm as Evan kissed Mavis's hand.

"D'you want to give me the parcel now?" she asked.

"If it's not too much trouble?"

"Of course not. Back in about five minutes, dear."

On his own, Mr Pringle listened to the music. The fountains rose and fell to a melody he recognized vaguely as of his own time and culture, plaintive but insidious. Was that all they could offer this beautiful land? Nothing but songs extolling a greed for sex? It seemed a poor return for all the pleasure he'd had today.

Chapter Six

They were lethargic next morning, heat had sapped the desire to do
more sightseeing. "Just a little stroll," Mavis declared; "that'll be
enough for me. Then a rest before we leave for the station." ·

As they stood on a footbridge above Petchburi Road watching
the lunch-hour chaos below she said, "He'll be half-way home by
now."

"Who, Evan?" Mr Pringle looked at his watch and tried to
grapple with time zones. "More than that, I think. He could be
landing soon." Mavis sighed.

"Odd, isn't it? On the other side of the world already and last
night we were all having dinner together. Nice boy . . . lovely
manners. Comes of having a Welsh mother, I expect." Mr Pringle
wasn't really listening. He was more interested in the lack of
aggression among Thai drivers despite the pressure of traffic. Had
London once been the same? He couldn't remember it.

"I need to go back and finish my packing," he reminded her.

"I did it for you while you were in the shower, dear. Let's find
somewhere that sells sandwiches. They warned us in the brochure
there might not be much food on the train."

There was only one coach-load for Bangkok station, the rest of the
charter having dispersed to Bali or, in the case of a quiet grey-
haired group, to one of the graveyards on the River Kwai. They
were, Mrs Bignell discovered, the only additional people accompanying the Friends of Nuclear Energy. She looked at her
fellow travellers disparagingly.

"Don't they look seedy? They wouldn't influence me—I don't
know about the Australians." Mr Pringle watched them climb
aboard. It was certainly true the group had a scruffy air and an
obstinacy concerning dress he'd observed before among the

39

British abroad. It was as if patriotism demanded they cling to flannel, collars and ties in spite of the tropical climate, to demonstrate a national identity. Unfortunately it made them a hot, unprepossessing bunch.

At the station, their leader checked off names on a list. "Pringle and ah . . . Bignell. Not members of our party, I think?" There was more than a hint of condescension.

"We're definitely not friends of nuclear energy if that's what you mean, so don't try and give us any badges," said Mavis firmly. The leader stared at her in horror.

"Madam—that information is classified!"

She returned his gaze, blandly. "Then you've had a little leak, haven't you? One of the sort your lot are always claiming can't happen."

It had taken longer than usual to pay in the bar takings at Crew Briefing because there was a queue. By the time Evan had finished and reached his old Metro in the pound, he was bone-weary. It was not only the time change with skin and mouth dry after hours of flying: he felt drained because of the irrevocable step he'd taken; there was no going back.

He hadn't slept during those few hours before the call came in Bangkok. He'd tried to convince himself there'd be no risk; nothing could go wrong. Mavis would do what he'd asked. By the time *they* found out, she'd be half-way across Australia.

Dare he risk driving to the cottage and having a shower? He desperately wanted to, and a pot of tea? No, no—for God's sake, what if he arrived too late? He had to get to London before those damn civil servants disappeared for the weekend. Panic made him grip the steering wheel—steady, steady . . . !

Evan threaded his way on to the roundabout and turned east along the M4. He wasn't going to the police. That would mean giving himself up. He'd be banged up in a cell as soon as he told them what he'd done and that would be the end.

But in Whitehall there was a department set up to protect citizens who found themselves in difficulties abroad. A liaison of civil servants to negotiate between the innocent and those foreign powers whom they'd inadvertently offended. If anything went wrong, Evan comforted himself with the thought, that department would rescue Mavis Bignell. Any niggling doubts he pushed to one side.

He would admit to them that he'd agreed to be a courier—"played along" was the way he'd describe it. He'd hand over the photographs as proof. It was essential to make them believe everything had been deliberate, from the beginning; a single-handed attempt to bring drug peddlers to justice. This last act involving Mavis Bignell was, he'd claim, born out of expediency just as he was preparing to make a clean breast of it. Until he'd forced the gang to send the photographs, he'd got no proof and once he had that, one false move and he was a dead man. The knowledge that he still could be made the sweat break out once more.

He'd hand over some of the money, that couldn't be avoided. He'd admit to three trips, that was all . . . he hadn't been foolish enough to pay all of it into the bank.

Everything depended on convincing Whitehall to set the necessary trap in Australia. Until that was sprung, Evan Jones would need police protection round the clock. A "safe house", that was what it was called. Somewhere with a bed where he could sleep for twelve hours!

He was breathing more easily, concentrating because of his tiredness, but with each mile growing in confidence. Stick to the plan, forget everything else; it was going to be all right.

The leader of the FONEs, a physicist, was called Protheroe. Once on the train, Mr Pringle managed to convince him Mrs Bignell meant no real harm by her remark. He bought the man a warm beer in the old-fashioned restaurant car with its windows wide open to the humid air.

Protheroe's shoulders were bowed down by the thousand and one irritations caused by herding colleagues plus their spouses on a good-will mission. Mr Pringle was sympathetic. He told of similar tribulations caused by citizens engaged in tax evasion. The physicist recognized a kindred spirit.

"One can't be too careful, Pringle. You see we haven't revealed the purpose of the mission to the Australian government, not yet. I don't mind telling you, that good lady of yours gave me a fright when she came out with the name like that. The trouble is, some of the wives in our party—they don't understand what the word 'secret' means."

"I don't think Mrs Bignell told anyone else . . ." Mr Pringle wondered about Evan but dismissed the idea.

"Thank God the sightseeing part is nearly over," complained Protheroe. "Tackling the natives is going to be tough as it is. The Australians are so *childish* about all things nuclear." It took another beer before Mr Pringle could excuse himself and return to the icy cool of their sleeper.

Mavis and he sat facing each other on the brown vinyl seats, watching lush vegetation slide past. The train travelled at a leisurely speed enabling them to gaze their fill at villages built on stilts, with walkways over irrigation canals, fringed by traveller's palms.

Occasionally they ambled through a station that might have come from some pre-Beeching line: single-storey, low-roofed, cream-painted with a verandah. In one, a saffron-clad monk helped dispel any notion they were back among the shires.

At dusk they went over a level crossing where children guarding water buffalo waved to them, and Mavis sighed with pleasure. "Isn't it wonderful," she murmured, "all those rice paddies and rubber plantations." Truth to tell, Mr Pringle was finding mile after mile of it soporific but wouldn't dream of saying so. The beer had left him feeling drowsy.

She examined the sleeping arrangements. "When they unfold these bunks, that top one's going to be a bit too close to the air conditioning for comfort. You'd better sleep down below, in mine." She gave him a knowing look. "I've always fancied trying it on a train, haven't you, dear?"

My word, he thought, twice in two days! He'd do his best, a man couldn't do more.

It had been several weeks since Anthony Pelham-Walker had experienced his revelation of futility. He'd almost given up hope. Five months to go to retirement and still nothing. He lay awake wondering if he dare beg his Maker for a dispensation; some small task that would give meaning to his life. They hadn't been in touch for years; had communications in that direction finally been severed?

But the boon was granted without a single prayer, delivered not by God's messenger but Crispin Sinclair. As he grasped its significance, Anthony Pelham-Walker felt his heart begin to pound.

Crispin wanted to scream; it was bad enough being caught just as he was leaving the office—but for Batman to sit reading the unwanted statement again and again . . .

"We should have handed him over rather than listen to him," Crispin said plaintively. "But the chap's Welsh. He charmed his way in then refused to budge until we'd taken it all down." Anthony Pelham-Walker looked up.

"What?"

"I'll telephone Scotland Yard, shall I?"

"Certainly not." No one was going to cheat him of this.

"I'm sorry, I don't quite follow . . . ?" Had Batman finally cracked?

"Jones came to us," Pelham-Walker insisted, "asking for our help—"

"But it's not ours to give, sir." Sinclair was shocked. "Quite frankly, the sooner we let the proper authorities have him, the better." He glanced furtively at his watch. He was going to miss the next train as well!

"These tourists, where are they now?" Crispin checked his notebook.

"Their train should reach Padang Besar in a couple of hours—which is why I really do feel we should contact the police."

"No!" Pelham-Walker was striding about the office. Crispin looked on helplessly.

"But what about the risk, sir? What else can we do?"

"Don't you realize what day it is, Sinclair, and the time?"

"Friday, sir. Twenty-seven minutes past six. Approximately."

"Exactly. We are the only ones left in Whitehall? Am I right?"

"Yes, sir, but in Scotland Yard there are lots of people—"
Anthony Pelham-Walker brushed this aside.

43

"He came to us," he repeated. "He wants *us* to intercede; that means you and I, Sinclair, or rather I alone. The matter is too delicate."

"Begging your pardon, sir, he wants us to act way outside our remit!" By way of reply, Anthony Pelham-Walker reached inside a drawer and flung his passport on to the desk.

"According to Jones's statement—" He picked up the paper again "—these tourists stay overnight in Penang before continuing to Singapore. After twenty-four hours there they fly to Sydney where Jones was due to hand over the package?"

"Yes." Crispin's eyes were drawn to the passport. What the hell was Batman up to? Forcing himself to look away he said, "Jones says he's made deliveries in Penang, Singapore and Sydney. Once he arrived there'd be a phone call to say where he should make the drop. They must have several couriers to keep the route supplied. Jones claims he doesn't know of anyone else but that's to be expected.

"In the normal way his roster for this trip would've included eight-hour stopovers at Abu Dhabi, Bangkok where he picked the stuff up—"

"From the dressing-table drawer in his hotel room," Anthony Pelham-Walker murmured. Crispin assumed this was a question.

"I think that has to be true, sir. Apparently, the crew are always allocated the same rooms in that particular hotel. Who better than a member of staff both to hide the stuff and keep tabs on the courier?" He took another furtive peek at his watch. "Don't you think—as time is not on our side, sir . . . ?" Anthony Pelham-Walker was once more engrossed in the statement.

"Jones states that he decided from the beginning to act—in the public interest—to bring these wicked men—"

"That's where the statement becomes a work of fiction, obviously," Crispin interrupted confidently. Pelham-Walker looked at him coldly.

"You think so? Tell me, is Jones not concerned for his own safety? After what he's done?"

"He's asked for police protection."

"He must have it, Sinclair. You must contact Scotland Yard and arrange it. As for the rest, that is down to me . . . What was the name of that tourist again?" Crispin gaped. "The name?" Pelham-Walker repeated curtly.

"Oh . . . Mavis Hilda Bignell. Jones saw her passport. Look, sir, don't you consider we should simply contact the duty officer. . .?" To his dismay, Batman shook his head.

"We are the correct authority, Sinclair. This department was created for this type of contingency." Anthony Pelham-Walker leaned across, full of enthusiasm. "It's why we must act!"

"You mean—send a telex?"

"Act, man, act! What good is a piece of paper? It didn't help Chamberlain."

"You don't mean . . . ?" Crispin Sinclair allowed the full horror to show on his face.

"Book me on a flight that connects with the one those tourists are catching out of Singapore."

"But what d'you intend to do?" Batman was transformed. He barked his thoughts like an actor playing Monty.

"Assuming this woman gets through . . . no reason why she shouldn't . . . Jones stresses she's no idea what's in the package, she'll behave innocently enough . . . She'll need protection only when she reaches Australia. That's when *they* will try and relieve her of it and where *we* will be waiting."

"We?"

"I. Plus the Australian police, of course. Notify them of my ETA and that we require their co-operation." He's loopy, thought Crispin, he's blown a gasket, gone round the twist, nutty as a fruit cake!

"Oh, and Sinclair—" Batman was wagging a finger "—that message must be in code. Any murmur outside these four walls and I shall hold you responsible."

It was late morning and the sun was at its zenith. It beat down from above and was reflected upwards from the concrete platform at Padang Besar. They waited, all of them crowded into the one small patch of shade by the Immigration shed. They had been told to leave the train while compartment doors were locked and Customs officers worked their way along the carriages, examining the luggage.

The heat was so fierce it had stopped all conversation; that, and the monster poster that faced them. Underneath a six-foot-tall hangman's noose, against a black background, the message was simple:

BE FOREWARNED
DEATH FOR DRUG TRAFFICKERS
UNDER MALAYSIAN LAW.

The same words, printed in red, showed up starkly on the immigration forms as, one by one, they shuffled closer to the metal grille to hand these over in exchange for the return of their passports. Protheroe, his head protected by a hanky, called out the names. "Mr G D H Pringle . . . Mrs M Bignell . . ."

They moved forward, pressing against the grille to be out of the sun. Official faces smiled in welcome. Mr Pringle smiled back and accepted his passport gratefully, tucking it away in his pocket. "Bignell, please . . . ?"

It wasn't the Immigration officer speaking, it was one of the uniformed Customs men. He called out again as he stepped down from one of the carriages, "Which one is Bignell?" Slung from his shoulder was Mavis's overnight bag. The zipper was undone; on top where everyone could see it was a square brown-paper parcel with an address in Byers Street, Enfield, Sydney NSW. "Open this, please."

Blood pounded through Mr Pringle's veins. The moment in time was frozen as everything became dreadfully clear. Something danced in front of his eyes, not spots but a hangman's noose over a gallows.

Ray Vincent was categorizing last year's house sales when the phone rang. It was the direct line. He heard the long-distance echo behind the familiar cough.

"It's OK, Janice, we can finish these later." As the girl glanced at the clock, he laughed. "Point taken. Why don't we tackle them first thing Monday?"

"Thanks, Ray." There was a swirl of skirt above the leather boots and she was gone.

Vincent murmured, "Hold on a moment," and listened. In the outer office there was the rustle of a mac, the word processor was switched off and the street door opened. As the Yale lock clicked shut, he murmured, "Yes?"

"Our reluctant friend didn't arrive at Singapore. His flight was changed."

"Shit!"

"Deal with it." That was all. Ray Vincent pushed the button for the dialling tone and tapped out a number from memory.

"Crew information?"

Evan had never felt so weary or exhilarated. They'd believed him, it was going to work! Provided Mavis wasn't picked up—and why should she be?—he was safe!

It was dusk; he switched on his headlights. He couldn't remember if he'd reset his watch when they landed this morning but what did that matter? It was nearly over.

The man in Whitehall had taken his statement then gone away to consult someone, presumably. He'd returned to ask for the photographs then, after another interminable wait, came back in a temper and told Evan to make himself scarce.

Excitement confused Evan. Had the man been sympathetic? He couldn't be sure. They were about the same age, him and the Whitehall bloke, but what different worlds . . . He shrugged as he thought of the sophistication and expensive suit. The man hadn't been particularly interested when Evan described where he'd be hiding. For Whitehall had been unable to offer protection even though Evan pleaded desperately.

"Go somewhere safe," the man kept saying. "Go sick, stay out of sight, you'll be perfectly all right. Leave a number where we can contact you."

Evan told him he'd be staying with Mam and gave the number of the chippy. He'd tried to make the product of a public school understand that in their street it was the only telephone. He'd had to repeat the number—excitement made his accent incomprehensible. Now he was on his way home, the safest place he knew.

He'd picked up details of his next trip at Crew Briefing: Cairo on the sixteenth. He'd collect a few things from the cottage then drive through the night to Carmarthen. On the sixteenth, if Whitehall gave him the go-ahead, he'd drive directly to Heathrow and pick up the flight. After tonight, he'd avoid the cottage like the plague until he knew it was safe, until he read in the papers they'd picked up the men in Sydney; that's when he'd be sure. In Whitehall, they'd promised to keep him informed. That chap had been decent; the more he thought about it, the more Evan was sure. It was going to be all right; he was free!

"What I still can't understand," said Mavis, "is why they were all such old books."

"So you said before," Mr Pringle answered shortly. Terror and heat had taken its toll. They had finished their train journey at Butterworth and dragged their cases the short sticky walk to the terminal. Now, on an ancient crowded boat belonging to the Star Ferry line, they were crossing to the island of Penang.

Mr Pringle hadn't had the courage to confess his imaginings at the Customs Post. As the wrapping had been torn off the parcel, he'd fainted clean away. People assured one another loudly it was because of the heat but when he'd opened his eyes, expecting to find Mavis in handcuffs, she'd been splashing him with eau-de Cologne. Beside her on the platform was a pile of worn paperbacks. After that, all Mr Pringle wanted to do was howl and disappear into a big dark hole—if only he could control his heartbeat!

Mavis waited placidly for him to recover. It was his own fault, she'd warned him often enough. At his age, she'd told him, you can't expect to be at it every night but whenever they went on holiday—would he listen? No, he would not. Serve him right. She hadn't felt like it in Bangkok because she'd been tired; she'd wanted the first time to be when they were on the train because it was so much more romantic. Like Somerset Maugham, she thought vaguely.

It was quite dark as Evan turned off the motorway and threaded his way through the lanes. He began to wonder if he would have left Singapore by now, had he been on the scheduled flight? It was too much effort to work out the time difference.

He looked hazily at the clock on the dash and noticed the red light shining fixedly. Christ, he must need petrol badly; it'd begun to flicker on his way into London. It made him nervous, wasting more time. He joked feverishly with the garage cashier as if needing to impress her with the memory of his visit.

He bumped down the track to the two cottages and switched off the engine. His next-door neighbour, an air-traffic controller at West Drayton, hadn't returned because his lights weren't on. Evan toyed with the idea of waiting in his car until the man reappeared but that was stupid. His neighbour might be working nights, not due back until the morning.

He must stop being twitchy. Grab clean jeans and some sweaters then drive like the clappers until he got to Wales. Brisk, eager to be on his way, Evan unlocked the front door.

Anthony Pelham-Walker told the car to wait; there was just enough time to pack a case before driving to Heathrow. As he approached the front door, he could see the lights were on; Fiona was having one of her parties.

Years ago the pretext had been furthering his career but once she'd realized she'd married a failure, Fiona dropped all pretence and invited her own friends instead.

It seemed to Anthony Pelham-Walker that every evening he returned to find his drunken wife making a fool of herself. He recognized it was partly his fault; she was disappointed in him. He hugged to himself the thought that all that was about to change, but as he ran downstairs, suitcase in hand, he felt compelled to drop one tiny hint. He was no longer the dull fellow she railed at, day after day; he had become—operational.

"I'm going outside, Fiona. I may be gone . . . some time."

"Well, piss off then!"

Chapter Seven

The elegant room in Penang, with its pale grey walls and silky bedcover, soothed them both. Below their private balcony the swimming pool beckoned. It didn't take Mr Pringle five minutes to get into his bathers but Mavis was trying on her new costume.

As he waited, he picked up one of the paperbacks that had shortened his life expectancy; a copy of *The Mousetrap* with a picture of the original London cast on the cover. He examined another by Nevil Shute. "I wouldn't have thought there was any problem buying these in Australia?"

"Neither would I," Mavis called from the bathroom.

"What d'you intend doing with them?"

"Sending them, like I promised. I've kept the wrapping paper and that's got the address on it. It shouldn't be difficult to parcel them up again . . ." She emerged. "What d'you think?"

"I say!" She'd talked about the bathing suit, described it as "an investment"—that meant she'd paid too much for it but all the same . . . "My word, Mavis!" Clinging fabric sculpted her body, lifting the proud breasts, emphasizing the surprisingly small waist, and burst into a cascade of emerald-green pleats over her milk-white thighs. Mavis smoothed the garment, satisfied.

"I think it was worth it."

"Worth it? You're a proper bobby-dazzler in that thing! Come on. I want to show you off to Protheroe."

In her painfully clean kitchen, Mrs Hardie made the first pot of tea of the day and let it brew. She took pride in her housekeeping. It was terrible the way Linda went about things. That mug, for instance. Ever since her daughter moved back in, Mrs Hardie had shut her eyes against its vulgarity—a naked woman's body with a handle on the back—disgusting! Mrs Hardie always used pretty china with a delicate honeysuckle design. It added to the flavour of the tea.

Pulling her sash tight, she picked up both mug and cup. Her quilted cotton dressing-gown was ankle length but the synthetic lining drooped lower. Taking care, Mrs Hardie began to climb the stairs. Behind her the letter-box snapped shut. A gaudy postcard, possibly from Mavis Bignell, fluttered down. Without thinking, Mrs Hardie turned, caught her foot and fell.

Scalding liquid soaked the quilting and burned her shoulder and breast. She lay very still, too sick to cry out, the picture of a Thai temple dancer on the floor beside her.

"Ma . . .? Oh God, what've you done!" Linda looked down on the fragile heap, one leg bent under at such an awkward angle. There was a flurry of cheap nylon lace as she ran downstairs. "What happened?"

"It was an accident. Ah!" Linda had attempted to lift her. "My leg!" moaned Mrs Hardie, "I think it's broken. I should've gone to that warden place when they offered . . . they've got no stairs there."

Crispin Sinclair's lover, a Grade Three at the FO, was having an extremely bad time. There was no doubt Big Bear was in one of his moods. Their weekend had been ruined. Big Bear got home too late for them to leave for the country and after that he'd spent the rest of the evening on the phone.

"What I bloody well can't understand is who's behind this charter," Crispin grumbled petulantly. "It sounds as if it's organized by British Nuclear Fuels but when I spoke to them, they denied all knowledge of it."

"Is it important?"

"Of course it is! Batman's on his way to Ockerland to join it. I'm supposed to send him the details—The Friends of Nuclear Energy, whoever they're supposed to be."

"Oh, you mean the FONEs." His Grade Three lover paused, the slice of toast half-way to his mouth.

"You've heard of them?"

"Yes but it's classified . . ." But his clearance was lower than Crispin's so it didn't take long.

Mavis sat in the shade by the pool with her new friend. They'd got as far as first names and photographs. "This is the little boy we're hoping to find while we're out there." Jean Protheroe resumed her glasses.

"You don't see many with rickets nowadays," she said. Mavis examined the photo more closely.

"His grandma never mentioned rickets."

"I think I'm right. I used to do health visiting . . . This is our conservatory, Mavis. Kenneth said 'Blow the cost, you only live once. Order whatever takes your fancy.'"

"Very nice!" The late Herbert Bignell had never made such an offer in his life.

At the deep end, Mr Pringle was equally fascinated by Protheroe's strategy for dumping nuclear waste.

"You say there are suitable sites already out there?"

"Yes, plenty. Quite big ones. What's more," Protheroe said cheerfully, "they're already contaminated. Where we tested the bomb in the fifties—remember?"

"Ah, yes . . . but doesn't the Australian government want Britain to go in and clean them up?" Protheroe shook his head vigorously.

"No point, none whatsoever. Cost us millions of pounds to do that—and why bother when we *need* somewhere for all our bally waste."

"But," Mr Pringle began tentatively, "won't the Australians object?"

"Thought of that." Protheroe was positively jovial. "Came up with a solution the Australians are bound to find acceptable." He whispered in Mr Pringle's ear, "Give the contaminated land back to the Aborigines!" Mr Pringle was mystified. "The black fellas are always demanding land," Protheroe explained. "They claim it was stolen from them in the first place."

"Yes, but surely . . . ?" Mr Pringle couldn't think of a tactful way of asking the question. "Won't there be a danger of—radiation?"

"Possibly." Protheroe measured his words judiciously. "One can't be one hundred per cent safe whatever the precautions, with nuclear waste." Mr Pringle saw he'd been misunderstood.

"What I meant was if the land is radioactive already and the Aborigines take it over, won't the Australian government be worried?"

"I doubt it." Protheroe was hearty. "I doubt it very much indeed. They never have been before."

Mr Pringle was speechless, but Protheroe called back as he splashed across the pool, "Killing two birds with one stone *and* making a profit—wouldn't be surprised if that isn't worth a gong in the birthday honours!"

In Farnham, Ray Vincent sat very still. Moonlight spilled over the desk and on to the floor. He'd have to leave the darkened office soon or Adele would begin to wonder. There was the telephone call as well, to New York, but for the moment everything was too much effort.

He'd called in here to scrub himself clean and shred his shirt and slacks. The scraps were in a box which he'd burn with the garden rubbish tomorrow. The light-weight jacket and trousers he'd changed into didn't keep him warm. Despite his efforts his body trembled in another spasm.

He was out of condition. He'd needed a Scotch before he left, another tumblerful when he got back. Automatically he reached to put the bottle back when he noticed the stains on the label. They were black under the moonlight but daylight would turn them red. He needed to stuff the bottle in the box with the rest. He hadn't the strength, his arms were leaden. "Come on, come on!" he muttered. The trouble was, the business wasn't finished.

"Your mother's worried about going back to your house which has stairs, that's the problem. She keeps saying she's had the offer of sheltered accommodation and wants to go there while she's still got the chance. Frankly, my dear, I'd jump at it if I were you. It's one of the few remaining ones that are run by the council. The rates are quite reasonable."

"No thank you, Sister. I'd much rather Mum came back home. I'll look after her."

Hospital visiting was nearly over and the sister still had her report to finish. All she should be concerned about was how soon they could discharge a patient. There was no reason to keep Mrs Hardie in provided she would be cared for.

"Are you sure you can manage? I know she's not heavy but your mother will need help with the lavatory for several days yet."

"Oh, yes." Linda forced herself to smile. "I'm sure she'd rather be at home. Among her own bits and pieces." Sister glanced at her watch.

"I'll talk to doctor about it." Most daughters would leap at the chance of subsidized, sheltered accommodation for a widowed mother. Should she point out the advantages once more? This woman looked as if she was the type for boyfriends rather than a stay-at-home. The bell rang for the end of visiting, putting a stop to their conversation.

Chapter Eight

The train arrived in Singapore at night and passengers queued to file past a dog behind a grille at the end of the platform. Three of them arrived together: Mr Pringle, Mavis and a student with a back pack. The dog barked suddenly. Mavis jerked to a halt and the other two cannoned into one another. The dog barked again.

"I shouldn't make a fuss of it," Mr Pringle warned, "it's probably been trained to bite." He watched in surprise. The dog was up on its hind legs, pawing frantically at the grille. "Hello? What's it doing that for?" Customs officers converged and within seconds the contents of the student's back pack were spread on the counter. Delicacy made Mr Pringle hold back; the young man's private life was no concern of his but an officer beckoned impatiently.

"I think they want us to go through, dear." They shuffled forward, close to the mesh. The wheels on Mrs Bignell's suitcase caught in the concrete and Mr Pringle bent to free them. Above his head the student was saying "There's only two left, for Chrissake!" as squashed sweet-smelling cigarettes were discovered in a jacket pocket.

Inches away from Mr Pringle's face, the dog barked frantically, saliva dripping from its jaws. He was offended. "I like dogs," he said, slightly hurt. He followed Mavis on to the concourse as the student plus back pack were ushered through an ominous-looking unmarked door.

In the taxi to the Orchard Hotel he was full of memories. "I used to have a tortoise when I was a boy . . . now those were difficult creatures to train."

"Perhaps that dog was hungry," said Mavis. "I know I am."

55

Singapore was bursting with wealth, full of fantastic buildings that looked as if they'd been put up only yesterday. After Bangkok, the contrast was startling. They left the bags and went in search of food. Orchard Road was full of skyscrapers and opulent restaurants. "D'you think we can afford to eat here?" Mavis shouted above the traffic.

"If we find somewhere modest . . . A little snack perhaps?"

Inside a hamburger bar, Mr Pringle grappled with the exchange rate. "Thank goodness we're not staying long!"

"Tomorrow morning we're going on a short tour of the city, including Raffles, then straight to the airport."

"Fine. I wouldn't mind an early night, either." But when they returned to the hotel, it was full of police: the Protheroes' room had been burgled.

Next morning, Mr Pringle asked, "Was much taken?" He'd felt diffident about joining the rest commiserating with the Protheroes over breakfast.

"Joan's not sure," said Mavis. "Everything was in such a mess. All their clothes chucked on the floor and trampled on—she was terribly upset. Hang on a minute, dear, I want to see how he does this."

They were in Raffles Hotel; they'd watched a scratchy video of the Japanese surrender set to Elgar. Now, in the Tiffin Room, an equally elderly bartender was demonstrating a gin sling. Mavis took a professional interest.

"Not that we have much call for those in The Bricklayers," she sighed, "but you never know."

On the aircraft to Sydney she had more news. "They've sorted themselves out and Joan doesn't think anything's been taken after all—isn't it odd?"

"Very. I bet Protheroe's upset."

"Oh, he is. He's convinced there's a mole from Greenpeace trying to sabotage their mission."

In England, there was another little leak of the sort that couldn't happen when the phone rang in Kenneth Protheroe's office. The voice was warm, Australian and male.

"Hi, this is Lenny. Coach captain on Wallaby Tours—'Hop with us from State to State' and all that. I'm phoning from Sydney, New South Wales, love." The amber nectar of his tone reminded Protheroe's secretary, Miss Wilson, of sunshine and everything else that was missing from her life.

"Yes?" she answered cautiously.

"Listen, love, this FONE party—any idea what it stands for?" Lenny asked innocently. "You see we got this logo on the side of all our coaches, it's a wallaby, right? And he's talking to a duck-billed platypus—and the point is, in the balloon sticking out of the wallaby's mouth, we like to put somethin' about our passengers, right?"

Miss Wilson understood. Not only that, Lenny's phone call had interrupted dark thoughts as to why her boss had been too mean to invite her to join the junket. There'd been plenty of spare seats.

"Last month we had 'On hire to the Rotarians of Toowoomba'," Lenny continued cheerfully. "We do it with big red stick-on letters, see, and I thought wouldn't it be nice if we could do somethin' like that for the Poms." He waited.

Serve Protheroe right, thought Miss Wilson savagely. Why shouldn't she be out there with this sexy Paul Hogan character instead of sitting here in a dingy office? There was a whistle in the earpiece. Minutes were ticking by on Wallaby Tours' phone bill. "Hi, darlin', you still there?"

No one had applied that word to Miss Wilson for years. "Have you a pen?" she asked.

In Macquarie Street, Kev asked, "Do you know what this is all about?" He waved the telex. Charlie shrugged.

"Some Pommie bastard comin' out on a free trip."

"Yeah, but why this particular bastard? This . . . Pelham?"

"Christ knows."

"And why," said Kev Macillvenny, aggrieved, "does the stupid so-and-so insist we turn out to meet him on a Sunday? Doesn't he know we got taxis in Australia? And a five-day week?"

*

57

Linda smiled brightly as she pulled up a chair. The metal legs scraped the polished vinyl. "I've brought you some magazines." They weren't the sort Mrs Hardie liked, with knitting patterns and recipes. "You'll never guess—I've managed to get the garden weeded ready for when you come out. It looks really nice now. You'd miss not having a garden, you know you would."

"I don't want no more stairs, Linda."

"Look, supposing I ask them at the bank . . . see if I can get a loan and have a lav put in downstairs, will that do?"

"But why can't I have a little flat? Sister says I'd get priority because of my accident. On the ground floor."

"Listen, Mum." Linda's voice trembled a little. She leaned forward so that other patients couldn't hear. "I don't want to leave while there's a chance Ben might come back. I want his room to be there, ready. I don't want the authorities pointing the finger, saying I haven't got anywhere suitable. You know they would if I was living in a one-bedroomed place. That's all I could afford if you give the house up."

"Why didn't you tell me that was the reason?" Mrs Hardie asked in surprise. Linda sniffed.

"I didn't realize you were that serious about the warden place, I suppose. Look, I'm sorry if things have been, you know . . . I'll try a bit harder when you come home, all right? Oh, this arrived today." Linda reached in her shoulder bag. "Mavis must be nearly at Sydney by now."

His private phone rang. There was the familiar echoey cough. "Just a minute." Ray Vincent closed the door to the outer office. "Yes?" His fleshy face was drawn, he'd lost his confident air.

"He didn't tell us everything . . ." Vincent swallowed. "They couldn't find it, Ray . . ." The caller waited for him to speak but he remained silent.

"We've told 'Parker' to meet you there . . ." This was a shock. Vincent tried to sound calm.

"OK."

"Make sure he tells you this time. . . before you deal with him." There was a click then the tone, so much louder than the whisper had been. Ray Vincent lit a cigarette and wasted over a minute smoking it before he opened the door and called, "Going to see a client about a property, Janice. Back by lunch time."

Chapter Nine

They flew in low over Botany Bay which seemed a bad omen. After they'd taxied to a halt, a granite-faced native leapt on board and sprayed them with tear-gas against contamination. Mr Pringle wondered nervously what other welcoming rituals awaited them in God's own country.

They passed through the usual formalities but Mrs Bignell's thoughts were elsewhere. As they emerged on to the concourse, he had to ask twice if she could remember the instructions concerning their coach.

"Oh, sorry, dear . . . I wasn't paying attention. According to the brochure it should be parked somewhere to the left once we get outside." She hesitated as if about to speak again but Mr Pringle was already moving towards the exit.

Lenny and Pete were on their hunkers in the shade. Their two vehicles proudly sported the new device. Against sparkling white paintwork, each wallaby told each platypus:

WE'RE TAKING
THE FRIENDS OF NUCLEAR ENERGY
ROUND AUSTRALIA!

Protheroe was the last to emerge. Others stood aghast. "Oh, no!" he cried. "No, no, no! Take that down at once!" Pete paused in rolling a cigarette.

"Isn't that typical?" he said in disgust. "All that work and them Poms aren't even grateful."

From the shelter of the building, Anthony Pelham-Walker watched them. He'd had plenty of time to regret his impetuosity. Between the Middle East and India he'd begun to draft his resignation on the back of a sick-bag but now, for the first time, he felt his spirits begin to lift. It was all turning out just as Evan Jones had prophesied, so why worry? Mavis Hilda Bignell had gone through Customs without any fuss. There she was now, climbing aboard the coach. All he had to do was tag along—and accept the plaudits afterwards. The Australian police would deal with any unpleasantness; he would simply sit back and wait.

He came to his senses; the first coach was ready to leave. Where was his own transport? Briefcase tucked under his arm, he stepped out from beneath the canopy.

Inside the Toyota, Kev Macillvenny said in disbelief, "That can't be him, can it? Not that dapper little nut?" Charlie groaned.

"Strewth! You gotta be jokin'?"

"Only one way to find out . . ." Kev heaved his bulk out of the car and strode across. "Mornin'. You Pelham? Hear you decided to pay us a little visit."

Anthony Pelham-Walker stared: shirt-sleeves? When the man was on duty? "I gather Sinclair managed to contact you," he said coldly. "Have you a car? We need to follow that coach."

The voice, like the attitude, was public-school insensitive, designed to put down all who heard it. It made Kev's toes curl and the hairs on his forearms bristle. "How 'bout puttin' me in the picture, Pelham? Just what the hell's goin' on?"

Pete and Lenny, supervised by Protheroe, removed some of the lettering. The sign now read:

WE'RE TAKING

THE

ROUND AUSTRALIA!

Pete was still resentful. "You lot don't have to worry 'bout secrets, not in Sydney. We know all about Pommie spies, we gotta book on the subject—"

"Once and for all, we are not members of MI5!" hissed Protheroe. Pete looked round the sweaty, travel-stained group.

"They should've told you back home, we don't *need* no more convicts—" Lenny grabbed his arm.

61

"Cool it, will you!" He gave Protheroe a tight, brief smile. "If you'd like to join your good lady, we'll get started," and shoved Pete towards the other coach.

"How was I to know he got no sense of humour?" demanded Pete. "Calls himself a Friend, don't he?"

In the Toyota, Anthony Pelham-Walker finished his explanation tiredly, "In short, a passenger aboard that first coach has, unknown to her, two kilos of heroin in her luggage."

"Bloody hell! And you let her take the risk of travelling with it?"

"Justifiable, in my opinion," he said defensively. "As you can see, she hasn't been picked up. Look out, they're off!" At the wheel, Charlie squirmed.

"Mister, we ain't rookies, you know." He slid into the line of traffic.

"What I don't understand, Pelham, is why you're here?" asked Kev. Truth to tell neither did Anthony Pelham-Walker any more. How could he explain to this huge man with the flabby belly the blinding self-knowledge that had brought him so low, or the certainty thirty-six hours ago that this voyage would bring fulfilment?

As a partial truth, could he plead extenuating circumstances? As it had been after four p.m. on a Friday, Whitehall had been empty and he the only suitable person available? Better not; that information was privileged.

"Why weren't we notified through the normal channels?" Kev persisted. "All we got to do is keep tabs on this lady and pick the guy up when he shows, right? Do we know anythin' else?"

"I've given you all the information we were able to glean," Pelham-Walker said curtly. "Don't let that woman out of your sight and we should learn the rest for ourselves."

Charlie smarted at the clipped authoritative tone: "Yes, sir!"

On the seventh floor of the Koala Hotel, Mr Pringle stood on the balcony, enchanted. "You can just see Sydney Harbour bridge—look!"

"Yes . . ." Mavis was unpacking their suitcases and sorting out laundry, but her thoughts were elsewhere. "You remember that dog, the one in Singapore?"

"What about it?"

"Do they always bark like that whenever there's the slightest trace of something?" A tiny cloud, no bigger than a man's hand, threatened Mr Pringle's sky.

"Why d'you ask?"

"When Evan gave me that parcel of books for his aunty, he remembered he'd brought her some flour as well. Stone-ground, wholemeal. You can't get it out here, apparently."

Mr Pringle felt dizzy suddenly and his knees began to buckle just as they had at the border post.

"Flour . . . ? Evan gave you . . . ?"

"Yes, in two plastic bags. I hadn't got room so I packed them with your things. The dog must have smelt it."

"Me! It was barking at me?" Mr Pringle was back inside the room, clinging to a chair.

"At your suitcase," she corrected. She caught sight of his face. "Don't get upset, dear, it's only flour. I didn't like to tell them their dog was barking over nothing, they might've been offended."

"Mavis—where's that 'flour' now?"

She lifted out his carefully folded shirts. There, at the bottom of the suitcase, between his sandals and *Hints On Camping For Scouts*, were two thick plastic bags, each full of a buff-coloured coarse powder. When he tried to speak, Mr Pringle found it difficult.

"How much would you say there was?"

Mavis considered. "They look the same as the ones I buy in Sainsbury's, about two pounds in each." She was puzzled by his expression. "You feeling all right, dear? Evan told me this flour was specially ground by someone he knew . . . his aunty has difficulty finding any."

"I'm not at all surprised," whispered G D H Pringle, hoarsely.

He'd been lying there so long, time had ceased to exist. Next door the air-traffic controller had come home and gone away again, back to West Drayton. There was no way Evan could attract his attention, his bonds were too tight.

The telephone wasn't the only red object in the room. There were splashes on the bare plaster and rolls of wallpaper. There was so much blood, a constant, dark red trickle, flies were buzzing in it.

He never knew there could be so much pain. His body was a screaming mass of agony. His brain couldn't cope, he kept fading in and out of consciousness, each shallow breath pushing death away ever more feebly. It couldn't continue: the will to live had nearly disappeared just as each gasp sucking in oxygen added to the endless pain, increasing the dark red wetness that oozed through the sodden rags.

He'd been so stupid, holding out like that—but then his plan had been stupid, too. He hadn't allowed for the snakelike speed of the organization when one of its members stepped out of line.

Evan had phoned his contact from Heathrow and recited the words he'd been practising all the way home. "When I realized I was on this terminator, I gave it to this tourist. She's tubby, reddish sort of hair, part of a charter travelling to Sydney. They're staying at the Koala—" His contact tried to interrupt at that point but Evan pressed on. "No, listen—*she* thinks I've given her a birthday present for my aunt—I gave her a parcel as well, with an address I copied off a pamphlet. All you've got to do is tell Sydney to collect the stuff. The charter arrives there Sunday so she can't post it." But his contact had phoned New York immediately instead.

It was so unfair! Only a few more minutes, he'd have been on his way to Wales. But the fair-haired bastard had got here first; he'd been waiting for him.

Throughout the tearing hacking at flesh and bone, Evan had clung to one idea: don't tell them everything. Keep something back. Give his saviours in Whitehall time to set the trap.

It wasn't saving him, it was costing him his life, that was the irony. They'd left him here to die. Slowly. Each time numbness forced him to move, the bleeding started up again, and the pain. . .

The axe was still there and beside it, thick with flies, two objects that looked like an old pair of gloves but which had once been a part of him.

And he'd thought he could cheat them! He was expendable. Three trips? There was no escape except death.

The door opened but Evan was no longer aware of sounds. It was the light across his face that made him open his eyes. There were two of them this time; the first, the one who'd done this to him, leaned over loosening the bonds. His pungent body odour was made even stronger by excitement. "Tell us the name this time or you'll die for it."

The second man was a thin black shape against the light. He giggled, high-pitched uncontrollable laughter. "We're going to show you what we do to naughty boys, holding out on us like that!" He moved closer and bent down so that Evan could see what he had in his hand—Oh, Mam! He'd tell them the name—Mavis Hilda Bignell—not that! Please!

It wasn't likely to be a long vigil outside the Koala Hotel but Kev and Charlie hadn't left anything to chance. They couldn't let this innocent Bignell dame risk her life. OK, so she'd been dumb, agreeing to help the steward like that, but she still had the right to protection.

It wasn't likely she'd be attacked. They'd wait until she and her partner were out somewhere then turn her room over. And boy, would that guy get a surprise! Charlie had three men posted on their floor.

Trouble was, this stupid Pom Pelham hadn't asked the steward the right questions. Charlie glowered at him in the driving mirror. Sleeping in the back, eyes closed, mouth open, twitching and making noises in his sleep. How could anyone criticize the Bignell lady when there were blokes like him in charge?

Charlie eased his spine against the back of the seat. One or two of the Poms had wandered past the parked car, guidebooks in hand. A notice in the foyer reminded all members of the FONE group their first meeting with the media was at six p.m.

Maybe whoever was coming to collect would assume Bignell would be attending it? Jesus, had they got to wait that long! Despite himself, Charlie yawned. He'd been planning a Sunday on the beach with an Esky full of cold Foster's.

From the back seat he suddenly heard the high plummy voice.

"There goes her friend, Pringle. According to Jones, he's not involved." They watched him wandering aimlessly, comparing the plan in his hand with the names of the streets.

"So why isn't she with him?" asked Kev.

"Perhaps she's taking a nap," said Pelham-Walker who badly wanted one himself.

"Oh, for Chrissake—look what he's carrying! Does he really think it'll rain?" Charlie's incredulity was loud.

"Why not? He's British," Pelham-Walker replied sharply.

She wasn't asleep, far from it, because they'd had a fearful row. Not the normal sort of tiff at all but a full-blown shouting match. Mavis still quivered at the memory. Despite the way the dog behaved in Singapore, she refused to accept Mr P's suggestion—it just wasn't possible, not with a nice boy like Evan.

She admitted to a soft spot: neither she nor Mr Pringle had children of their own and sometimes Mavis experienced maternal yearnings. On this occasion it had been those blue eyes, the way Evan had smiled at her and his lovely manners. He'd looked so smart that day in Bangkok. Mrs Bignell also had a weakness for short-sleeved stripy shirts with buttoned-down collars; Mr Pringle thought they were cissy.

But it wasn't as if Mr Pringle knew for certain—he was as ignorant as she was. Even when they made a tiny hole in one of the plastic bags, he couldn't be sure what the stuff was. Mavis was furious at the injustice of it. He hadn't let her sniff or taste, he said that would be far too dangerous. Admittedly the powder had got a funny sort of smell, but that was all. As neither of them went in for all that health food nonsense, who was to say it wasn't wholemeal stone-ground flour? She pushed aside her doubts. If it came to choosing between a barking mongrel or Evan Jones, the boy got her vote every time.

Mr P had marched off without apologizing, to get rid of it. He'd tried pouring some down the lavatory but the smell had made them queasy. It still lingered even though they'd opened the windows. Fortunately, there was a breeze which ought to do the trick. Mrs Bignell sat at the dressing-table pondering what to do next.

It was a nuisance, discovering it was a Sunday. There were postcards to send as well as the parcel. She looked at it, idly; Byers Street, Enfield, Sydney. "I wonder if they've got a tube or buses," she thought; then more vigorously, "If they have, I'll damn well take it there myself. His aunty's going to have one present on her birthday."

Mr Pringle wandered along Oxford Street and into an empty commercial quarter. He'd solved the problem of carrying the powder easily enough. He never travelled without a plastic mac. It was dun-coloured as its predecessor had been and the one before that. It had been bought at the same gents' outfitters he always patronized and if the design had varied one iota from the first mac Mr Pringle had purchased there in 1949, he would've been dumbfounded.

Like all the others, it had two large pockets with flaps. While Mrs Bignell scoffed, Mr Pringle put a plastic bag of 'flour' in each, securing the flaps with Sellotape from his camping kit. He'd refolded the mac neatly so the bulging pockets didn't show and announced his intention of taking a walk.

"If anyone asks, you can tell them I have the powder. That should ensure your safety." As he'd said this he'd felt incredibly noble.

"The only one who's likely to, is a little old Welsh lady who's been looking forward to a few wholemeal scones!" Mavis replied derisively.

At first, he'd toyed with the idea of dropping both bags into some municipal waste-bin, but dismissed it. Their fingerprints were all over the plastic and besides, that wouldn't destroy the stuff. Mr Pringle intended to get rid of it once and for all. As to what would happen when the traffickers found out . . . terror blurred his vision and made him stumble.

Anger had faded. He shouldn't have shouted. It wasn't in Mavis's nature to be disloyal and she believed in Evan Jones. If Mr Pringle hadn't been so tired—or frightened—he might have behaved more rationally. Fear dominated him now, making him glance back over his shoulder.

Those men in the car outside the hotel had given him a scare but they hadn't looked up. He'd armed himself with Mrs Bignell's camera to look more convincing as a tourist—if only his knees would stop wobbling! Perhaps the disguise was unnecessary? None of the passers-by turned to look. Mr Pringle concluded, not for the first time, that he really was the sort of chap other people ignored.

He passed an attractive modern building with a fountain, but hurried on when he saw it was a law court. He was descending rapidly towards the harbour. Between him and the water were trees, some sort of park. Mr Pringle walked into the Botanic Gardens, looking for somewhere to dispose of the powder, and ahead, against a perfect sky, he saw the unmistakable silhouette of the Sydney Opera House.

He was thirsty. It was hours since the last plastic cup of orange juice on the aircraft. He climbed the long flight of steps with the rest of the visitors and walked round the outside, admiring the silvery white domes despite his worries. On the far side, built out over the harbour, was an open-air café with tables, chairs and umbrellas. Children were eating ice-cream; their parents had pots of tea! In an instant Mr Pringle had joined the queue.

He sat at a table nearest the railing. If only he could empty the two bags into the harbour . . . but he could, couldn't he? Provided he was careful, what was there to stop him? The first seagull landed on the chair beside him.

It was the biggest bird he'd ever seen, until the next one joined it. Mr Pringle looked around; there were seagulls everywhere, huge, red-eyed monsters, swooping on titbits before customers had finished eating, arrogant bird-terrorists demanding ransoms.

Mr Pringle had never liked gulls. These terrified him. Never mind, they couldn't interfere. Summoning his courage, checking to make sure no one was watching, he took out his pocket-knife. He made a couple of slits through the pocket into the bag and began to shake the contents into the bay.

For her little outing, Mrs Bignell dressed in her floral two-piece. It was bright, herbaceous and gave her courage. She needed a bit of that, on her own in a strange town. But they'd been ever so helpful downstairs. One of the receptionists had taken her outside, and explained the route. Now she was on her way to the railway station at Circular Quay.

"That's her," said Pelham-Walker suddenly.

"You mean—that seed-packet lady?" Charlie asked.

"Yes."

Kev was older than Charlie and his tastes were more mature. He gave a deep-throated, appreciative growl.

"Look—she's off somewhere. We'll have to do something soon or we'll lose sight of her!" cried Pelham-Walker. Kev swallowed a retort.

"She's not got the stuff," he observed calmly. "That handbag's too tiddly, unless it's the parcel, but that looks too small as well—"

"She's getting away!"

"Think you can manage all by yourself, Charlie?" Kev smirked.

"Aw, shove off!"

Thank God none of the fellas were around to watch him tail a red-haired woman dressed in all the colours of the rainbow—it was embarrassing!

Enfield was further than Mavis anticipated. After the city, Sydney suburbs were monotonous, nothing but mile after mile of bungalows interspersed with shops. Some slums, too; she hadn't imagined there'd be any of those in Australia. Never mind, the weather was gorgeous.

Wanting to be friendly, Mavis remarked on this to a fellow passenger. The woman stared before saying as it had bloody well been the same for the past nine months, when did *she* think they could expect a decent drop of rain? Which just went to prove, thought Mavis philosophically, some people are never satisfied . . . All the same, her feet were killing her. She'd definitely take a taxi back.

The bus journey was more interesting. One or two of the shop-fronts reminded her of childhood holidays in south coast resorts, queuing up for Liguorice Allsorts. Apart from the weather, she could've been back in England—"Byers Street!"

There were single-storey dwellings as far as the eye could see. One or two were old-fashioned, clapboard built with faded ochre corrugated roofs. Mavis checked the number on her parcel—it was the green-painted wooden one with that huge tree in the front garden. She walked up the three steps and, in the absence of a bell, rattled a rusty fly-screen.

Charlie watched. Mrs Bignell grew impatient. She checked the number against the one on the parcel and rattled the screen again. After another pause she walked along the verandah, peering in at the windows. "Lady, I hope you know what you're doin'," Charlie breathed. He waited until she'd disappeared round the side of the house before running like crazy to the end of the block, down the next street and vaulting over a locked gate—he was in the grounds of some clubhouse. Keeping low, Charlie covered the scrubby grass at speed and peered through a crack in the boundary fence. The Bignell woman was at the back of the property now, shouting through a half-open door. From where he stood, Charlie could hear: "Hallo? Are you there? I've brought a birthday present from Evan."

The breeze was much stiffer now, whirling rubbish in among the white tables and chairs. The Sunday visitors had gone, including the man who'd sat beside the rail. Only the waitresses remained to witness the kamikaze gulls. "Did you ever see anything like it? Look at that, I don't believe it! That bird dived straight into the water!"

"It must've broken its neck?"

"Yeah, I reckon—hey, what about those two, ripping each other's feathers out?"

"Jacqui, over there! On that table!"

"Oh, my God, what a mess!" As the sun went down leaving only cold and darkness behind, they continued to watch the mayhem, unable to tear themselves away.

Mr Pringle arrived back first. He sidled past the open door where Protheroe was conducting the meeting and into the lift. He too had a peace offering: a bottle of brandy. In their room, he found Mavis's note: "Gone to deliver parcel. Back soon."

G D H Pringle's blood ran chill in his veins. She still refused to accept the truth and had gone to meet those drug traffickers, face to face. Why, they might even now be torturing her! Images flashed past, each worse than the last, of all Mr Pringle had read of their dreadful practices. He must phone the police! If they went immediately, they might still be in time to save her. The address? What was the address on the parcel?

He seized the waste-basket but it was empty. Mrs Bignell had used the same wrapping after all. He racked his tired brain but couldn't remember any of it, not even the name of the street. As he stood there, impotent and helpless, tears began to fall. "Oh, Mavis . . . !"

Behind him, the door rattled impatiently. "Open up, dear. It's me, I'm back."

"She was out anyway."

"If she ever existed."

"I left the books. And a note."

"Did you mention the flour?" he asked anxiously. Mavis shook her head.

"I thought I'd better not, to be on the safe side. Mind you, I still don't believe you but I want to give Evan a chance. I'm going to write to him."

"All right." He'd agree to that, for the sake of reconciliation. Both were of an age and sensibility to know how important this was, not to be hurried nor glossed over in trite phrases.

Mr Pringle wondered again whether he should stress how cruel drug traffickers could be. Mavis looked so relaxed, sitting there in her pretty dress, drinking brandy, why spoil the mood? Besides, he could explain to the police if the need arose.

"It definitely wasn't flour," he insisted weakly. "You should've seen what it did to those gulls!"

"Yes, well, if anyone does turn up we can tell them there's a whole new lot of addicts flying round Sydney harbour."

"Mavis, it may not be that simple. Drug dealers are extremely ruthless! Two kilos of heroin or cocaine, whatever it was, must represent an enormous sum of money—"

"Serve them right," Mavis countered stoutly.

"Mavis—" His small stock of courage had ebbed away "—let's tell the police now, for our own protection?" She shook her head.

"No. We've got to give Evan a chance. I'm going to write to him

71

at his mam's and tell him if he has been led astray, he's got to go straight from now on. I'm not going to tell him we've got rid of the flour—he's more likely to take my advice if he thinks we've still got it and could hand it over to the authorities."

"I hope you're right." Mr Pringle was much less sanguine. "What did you say in your note?"

"I wrote it in Welsh," she said smugly. "If his aunty really does live there, she'll understand."

They puzzled over Charlie's copy of it in Macquarie Street: "MANY HAPPY RETURNS, YACKYDA, FROM A FRIEND OF EVAN!"

"So what does it mean, Pelham?"

"I've told you, I haven't the least idea," he repeated for the twentieth time. Kev picked up the list of titles.

"Forensic are checking the books. If it's a code, let's hope they can break it. Why don't you phone your office, Pelham? Tell 'em to put the pressure on Jones? Get some results for a change."

Anthony Pelham-Walker's petulant mouth set in an obstinate line. "There's absolutely no point in telephoning before ten a.m. Monday at the earliest—"

"Jesus wept!" muttered Charlie. Kev left an eloquent pause.

"So all we got," he said eventually, "is two facts: number one, she's still got two kilos in her luggage; and number two, no one's made contact yet—check Charlie?"

Charlie shook his head emphatically. "No phone calls, no one visited the room. We know she didn't have nuthin' with her this afternoon except that parcel and a tiddly little purse . . . It's still got to be there."

"And she's got to be protected."

"Right," Charlie agreed.

"What happens now?" Anthony Pelham-Walker demanded. "It was my intention to be on the return flight this evening. I really can't go on sitting here, waiting for something to happen . . ."

Kev glared and he shrivelled into silence. "If you want to get on the flight, Pelham, be my guest. I'm telling the truth when I say Charlie and me would be glad if you did . . ." He waited hopefully but Pelham-Walker made no reply. "However," Kev continued, "if you want to stay with us instead, I suppose we can't stop you doing that either."

Anthony Pelham-Walker had every intention of staying. What was the point of returning empty-handed with the additional problem of explaining away two thousand pounds of tax-payers' money wasted on a ticket to Australia? Realizing Pelham wouldn't budge, Kev turned his back and consulted Charlie instead.

"What's their itinerary?"

"They're coach-camping with these FONE people as far as the Red Centre. After that, the party splits up."

"It'll take a few days to get that far. Know what I reckon? As they haven't made the pick-up here in Sydney, I guess the plan is to do it somewhere quiet, on one of the campsites. It'd be so easy to rob a tent, some place where there weren't too many police around." Charlie nodded.

"So we go along?"

"Right. The Bignell lady still has the stuff but she doesn't know what it is. We'll have to assume that Jones told her to leave that message at Byers Street—who lives there anyway?"

"An Asian couple. Seems like they're away for the weekend." As Kev raised his eyebrows, Charlie nodded in agreement. "Could be a lead. We're checking on it. Meanwhile—" He jerked his head "—which of us gets to share a tent with him?"

Chapter Ten

"What I'm looking forward to now, apart from seeing the countryside of course," said Mavis, "is finding Mrs Hardie's grandson." Hope sprang as optimistically as ever after a good night's sleep.

Mr Pringle didn't share it; he'd had nightmares, full of terrifying images of dead seagulls, torn and bleeding, floating in Sydney harbour. He'd also woken to the certain knowledge that someone, somewhere, would come in search of those two plastic bags.

"According to the brochure," Mavis reminded him, as they walked towards the lift, "we can start the search for Ben today. We're due in Bathurst for lunch."

Anthony Pelham-Walker, too, was feeling sombre. The spurt of energy which had caused him to leave England precipitately had disappeared, leaving cold reality behind. He'd behaved irrationally and that wouldn't be forgiven in Whitehall.

As he shaved, he tried to analyse and quantify. He'd assumed could he but witness the hand-over of drugs, protect an innocent female and order the arrest of the unknown malefactor, he could return in triumph. How childish! And look what it had cost? In an era of ministerial purges when expenses were being cut through the bone to the marrow! He might be close to retirement but he'd be lucky to hang on to his pension after this!

There was a thud against the door. He opened it and picked up the newspapers. If he'd felt doom-laden before, today's headlines made him suicidal:

"POMS TO DUMP RADIOACTIVE MUCK HERE!"
"AUSSIES SAY 'NO' TO BRITS' NUCLEAR WASTE!"
"GET OUT AND STAY OUT—FONES' COVER BLOWN!"

Comprehension was swift. "Oh, Lord," muttered Anthony Pelham-Walker. His predicament had got worse. Never mind trying to creep back home and explain, far better disappear into the outback for a while until the fuss had died down.

Jean Protheroe, white, shaken, told them about the newspapers. "It's brought on Kenneth's asthma!" she whispered. "I'm going up to our room to find his inhaler." Mavis was mystified.

"Surely everyone guessed the idea might not be popular?"

In the dining room, scientists gathered in anxious groups. Understanding had penetrated even the most academic: here in Australia, the natives didn't want to glow in the dark.

Mr Pringle read the headlines. He didn't care what happened to Protheroe. If the FONEs wanted to split atoms, they should take responsibility for cleaning up the bits afterwards. He reached the back page and sighed with relief: not a word about dead gulls polluting Sydney harbour!

As he sipped his coffee a much comforting thought occurred: if Protheroe had succeeded in alienating the locals, maybe the police would travel with the coach, to protect the party? Oh yes, that was a lovely idea! That way he and Mavis would be completely safe.

Mrs Hardie was awake. They'd dimmed the lights but she hadn't taken the pill to make her sleep. The ward was quiet. Nearer to the nursing station, an accident victim moaned despite the drugs. She'd have plenty to cry about once she saw herself in a mirror, thought Mrs Hardie sympathetically.

Beside her locker, the suitcase Linda had brought was packed ready. All she had to do in the morning was put in her nightdress and washing things. The crimplene trouser suit and frilly blouse were on the chair; tomorrow, Mrs Hardie was going home.

Although eager, she kept remembering the conversation with the welfare lady. Yet again Mrs Hardie had turned down the offer of a flat. "I can't keep promising you one," the woman told her worriedly. "I don't know when there'll be another."

It was true. Occupants at Brierly Court often found a new lease of life inside the comfortable well-planned flatlets. "There'd be companionship," the welfare lady told her. Mrs Hardie understood:

Linda. She was going back to sharing with her daughter. It hadn't worked before. If it didn't this time, Mrs Hardie might be stuck with it.

She hadn't been fair, she told herself. Look what her daughter had had to put up with? Most girls would've gone off the rails, losing Ben and Gary at the same time. And Linda was making the effort these days. She'd visited at least three times. She'd cleaned the house, ready for the home-coming. The living-room sofa had been turned into a bed, the hospital was lending a commode and she'd promised to look after her mother.

"I shall manage," Mrs Hardie told herself; "I owe it to Linda to try again. Anyway, we'll have to stay put, so Ben'll have a place when Mavis brings him back."

Their departure from the hotel had been quick and furtive. Scientists scurried out, convinced that hordes of Australians were after their blood, but the street was empty. It was early and the public hadn't had time to react. Rather embarrassed, removing dark glasses and turning down their collars, the Friends of Nuclear Energy took their seats. Mr Pringle and Mrs Bignell were half-way down Pete's coach. Each day passengers would rotate, Lenny ordered, thus everyone got a turn in the front seat. Protheroe had objected. He'd assumed that seat was his.

Today, apart from Lenny and Pete, plus a trainee driver, there was also the cook: Sheri. She would accompany them throughout the journey, Mr Pringle learned, and he thought this an excellent idea. Sheri was nubile, she wore a sleeveless T-shirt and very short shorts. Much of her golden flesh was available to admire. Not that he was being disloyal to Mavis. Memories of their quarrel were still vivid—he was anxious not to upset *her* in any way—but a little variety never did anyone any harm, especially at his age.

The sight of tightly rolled sleeping-bags above their heads was exciting. In the bowels of the coach behind their luggage were the tents. How would he compare with his fellow explorers once they were out in—The Bush?

Mr Pringle's emergency camping pack was with his pyjamas: penknife, coiled twine, needle and thread, spare tent-peg, matches, candle, torch including spare batteries, a twin-pack of soft lavatory paper (pink, in deference to Mrs Bignell) and last, but most important of all, his old scouting manual—G D H Pringle was prepared. He wouldn't mind betting the nuclear physicists weren't. The ability to blow up the planet didn't necessarily equip a man for survival on its surface.

From her window seat, Mavis's contentment increased with every kilometre. The air was so clean and sparkling out here, as if someone had peeled away the dirt and damp; she could see for miles. They drove out of Sydney, past graceful small terraces with ornamental iron balconies. These gave way to industrial suburbs but as they reached Parramatta elegant houses began, surrounded by trees and paddocks. The highway narrowed and began to climb. In the distance she could actually see the Blue Mountains!

Pete had read the morning papers. He didn't like the sound of this party at all. These bloody Poms wanted to screw up Australia! "Mornin' folks. Like to tell you about the amenities on the coach. You'll have noticed the toilet down the back. It's got chemicals in it. Right now, it's clean. If it gets used, we've got to add more chemicals . . . which is OK in New South Wales, we got modern roads. Further out, Stuart Highway for instance, the surface is really bad. Full of holes. But that toilet is there for your convenience, if you really need it. Once we're in the bush, we use a gunny shovel. That's G-U-N-N-Y, for shovelling shit."

Behind him, in the Wallaby Tours uniform of dark red shorts, navy socks and white open-necked shirt, Charlie grinned. The badge on his pocket described him as a trainee-driver. As far as Lenny and Pete were concerned, he'd been put there by the government to keep an eye on the FONEs. Pete gave it as his opinion that this was a bloody good idea. Charlie waited for the next titbit from Pete. From their faces he could see that a few of the passengers were beginning to revise any romantic notions about the outback.

Pete changed the subject. He'd made them anxious about their bladders, now he wanted to stir them up a bit. "This trip's nice and easy, folks," he announced ruminatively. "Plenty of spare time in the schedule. Maybe we could make a detour, visit those contaminated sites you're interested in. . . Would you like that?"

There was a worried consultation down the back, a pretence at examining maps and itineraries. It was one thing to describe radioactive land as "suitable for our purpose", none of them had envisaged setting foot on it. Naturally it would be perfectly safe, they told each other, but that was no reason to change the route. Pete watched through his driving mirror. "Just testing," he murmured.

Protheroe seized the mike and reminded them the great camping adventure would begin in earnest tomorrow. Tonight would be their last in a comfortable bed, in a motel in Coonabarabran.

They were climbing higher and higher. On either side, skeletal-grey eucalyptus, the bark hanging in shreds, framed the vastness beyond: from horizon to horizon, nothing but thickly wooded mountains. Above the tree-tops in the heat, the blue gum haze merged into an infinity of sky.

"Big, isn't it?" said Mavis. Bigger than she'd expected; had *Reader's Digest* misled her? Surely not?

In the Toyota, Anthony Pelham-Walker gazed uneasily at the view. He'd telexed the necessary instructions to Sinclair before they left, to proceed immediately to Wales and contact Jones. So far the scientists here had been unable to fathom the message. And Charlie had drawn a gloomy blank in Byers Street.

"Couple got back in the early hours . . . Japanese. Missionaries. It's church property, rented out to whoever needs it. We've checked them out." Kev snorted.

"If Jones knew Byers Street was in Enfield, maybe he'd made drops at another house?" He and Charlie had looked at Pelham-Walker and he'd been forced to admit that Jones hadn't been asked the question.

"I—we didn't enquire about—drops."

"Jesus—didn't you ask him anythin'?" Kev demanded.

How could he defend his lack of expertise? Of course he hadn't known what questions to ask, his department weren't interested. Their task was to extricate stupid fools like Jones from foreign jails then hand them over to the police. *They* did the questioning.

Anthony Pelham-Walker felt himself shrinking, like Alice. He had to assert himself or he'd fall down the nearest rabbit hole. "I think," he said slowly, "I should have gone on the coach, rather than Charles." Kev shifted the gum in his mouth.

"You handle a gun, Pelham?" The shock made him gasp. "You don't mean—he's armed?"

"What d'you think this is, for Chrissake? A picnic trip? Those people want their drugs back, they want to stop the rot started by Jones and if that Bignell lady gets in their way, they'll try and kill her."

The two coaches drove in convoy into Bathurst, past spacious properties. Horses grazed in outlying fields but the town itself was small and compact. Both Mavis and Mr Pringle, still making comparisons with England, expected a city. "Bathurst ends at the bottom of that street," said Mavis in surprise indicating the burnt brown–grey plain. "It's amazing how wide the roads are considering that's all there is."

"Wide enough for a bullock cart to turn." Mr Pringle had been reading the literature.

"Oh, look! There's the place!"

The coaches had pulled up beside open parkland in the centre where Lenny told them they would picnic. It was at the main intersection and as he looked in the direction of Mrs Bignell's hand, Mr Pringle found himself gazing at the view on the postcard.

There were the same stubby lamp-standards down the middle of the street, their white globes like giant blobs of ice-cream, the same cars parked at an angle to the kerb and, on the corner facing them, the ice-cream parlour itself. It was as immaculate, clean and shiny as the postcard and Mr Pringle, having come so far, blinked to discover it was real.

"What d'you want to do?" he asked awkwardly. He hadn't discussed tactics. All along he'd thought it so unlikely they'd find the parlour; he hadn't allowed for the Australian scale.

Bathurst looked sizeable on the map because for many, many miles there was nothing but isolated farms. It was definitely a town, however, the hub of a widely spread community, full of shops, churches, pubs and services, sheltering from a midday sun under canopies that stretched out over the pavements.

Beside the coaches, Protheroe was organizing a queue: lunch

79

was nearly ready. It had been a smooth operation. Lenny and Pete put up tables, Sheri set out salad and fruit. On a portable grill, hamburgers were sizzling. Breakfast was a distant memory and Mr Pringle discovered he was peckish.

"Shouldn't we eat first?" he suggested feebly.

"Eat?" Mavis stared. "After coming all this way? We're going over there to ask questions and show them Ben's photo. You can have a cornet if you're that hungry."

"Hallo . . . ?" Charlie shielded his eyes. "Take over for me will you, mate?" Pete flipped the hamburgers expertly.

"Come and get it, folks. Grub's ready."

Chapter Eleven

Rain swept across in sheets, rippling over the pavements and filling the gutters. It washed the fronts of the houses, the sash-windows, the steps up to the inset front doors and ran down the brickwork. It poured endlessly on to black roofs making the slates gleam, but the sheer volume of water couldn't eradicate the hopelessness; it was a desolate place.

Crispin Sinclair watched sullenly as the torrent blotted out the view. Reaction in Whitehall this morning, when they'd discovered what Batman had done, ranged from incredulity to complete indignation, but to Crispin's shocked surprise the guns had been turned on him as well. Why hadn't he reported what was going on? Why fall back on the lame excuse of "acting under orders"? Why not use his initiative? Or hadn't he got any? His answers had obviously been judged unsatisfactory and the remainder of the interview was equally unpleasant.

Now he'd been ordered to sodden old Wales to rescue his reputation because of that stupid telex from Sydney. What was worse, if he didn't succeed in squeezing every last scrap of information out of Jones, it would count against him at his next assessment. Damn and blast!

Crispin peered through the windscreen: what a place! No wonder Evan Jones preferred to travel. He switched the wiper to its fastest speed and looked along the row of houses. They were all so—neglected. People should make an effort to help themselves, he thought irritably. A few thou' spent on refurbishing and this street could be transformed. You saw it happen in London all the time.

He started the engine and coasted along, pulling up short of the actual house. Living rooms fronted directly on to the pavement. Through several windows he could see televisions with bodies slumped in front of them, watching endless rubbishy movies. In the middle of the afternoon! Crispin's antipathy increased. Why not get out and do something? Pulling his belt tight, he made a dash for the drab front door.

"Yes?" The girl was about twenty and the resemblance to Evan was strong. Hair fell across her forehead in the same dark wave, the eyes were blue but what a pallor she had. No international traveller this. She hugged the shapeless cardigan protectively across her breast. "Yes?" she asked again.

"I'd like to see Evan Jones if he's at home."

"Evan?" She looked blank. Crispin experienced a flash of anger: had the idiot given a false address?

"Evan Jones," Crispin repeated as to a half-wit. "He's an airline steward. I understand his family live here?"

"Yes, we do but Evan isn't home. He's away somewhere." Blast! Rain was seeping in through Crispin's fashionable Italian leather shoes.

"Look, d'you think I could come inside? If Evan isn't here, I'd like to speak to his mother instead." The girl was shivering and doubtful. "Here's some identification . . ." Crispin fished out his driving licence and staff pass. The girl shrank even further from the official-looking stamp.

"You can come in, I suppose. Mam's out. It's Monday. She's down the Social Security."

He waited in the dank front parlour. In this house the television was in the kitchen-cum-dining room at the back. He caught a quick glimpse as the girl opened the door from the passage on her way to make tea. He saw people look up—there were four or five in that back room but none of them was Evan Jones. The ceiling light was on. It emphasized the gloom beyond the window and shone on their pale expressionless faces.

Crispin Sinclair retreated to the unlived-in parlour. What purpose did the room have? An uncut moquette suite, regimentally placed, and a battered upright piano with lacy material draped over the top. There was even a metronome—did anyone ever play? Everything reflected an earlier era, especially the furniture, obviously deemed too good to be thrown away. The room would never be used but held in readiness for Christmas or funerals.

Everything was too damn clean. His shoes had already left marks on the semicircular rug; he could scarcely take them off. There was nowhere to put them except on the hearth. A few spots of soot sullied the tiles, washed down in the deluge, proof there had once been a fire. Like the girl, Crispin shivered. Probably no heat in here since last Christmas. The grate was filled with red paper roses.

"Two sugars, you said?"

"Please."

"I'm sorry, there aren't any biscuits."

"I'm not hungry. Really." As soon as he'd finished here, he'd find the best hotel and have the largest steak on the menu. He smiled. "Lovely cup of tea." She didn't respond.

"Why d'you want Evan? There's nothing wrong, is there?" Her twenty-year-old face looked suddenly older, as if expecting trouble.

"I met him recently. We had a chat. As I was passing through Carmarthen . . ." That was a mistake. Nobody "passed" by this street. He saw her withdrawal. "Well, to be honest, Evan told me all about his 'mam'." Crispin tried to make the imaginary conversation sound warm and intimate. "Said if I was ever anywhere near here, to come and look her up." The girl was still dubious.

"I can give Mam a message if you like?" Crispin smiled again.

"I knew you must be Evan's sister, but no, thank you. I'm not in any hurry. Tell me, where d'you think he might be?" She shrugged.

"Mam might know. I can't remember. I think she said it was Bangkok this time, or Hong Kong. Somewhere out there." The girl couldn't care less; she'd as much chance of seeing either city as flying to the moon.

"When I met him in London, a few days ago, Evan had just returned from Bangkok." It wasn't any good, he couldn't interest her in that. "Doesn't he come back here between trips then?" Crispin asked casually. "I remember him mentioning that he did."

"Sometimes. He's got a house near London. Near the airport, anyway. He's doing it up. He says we can go and stay with him when it's ready." There was a little animation at the thought of the treat. "Evan's there more often than here because of getting it straight."

If he was there now, he was being plain bloody stupid, thought Crispin contemptuously; at least in this tight community he'd have had the protection of his family. Should he cut his losses? It was obvious the steward hadn't come back to Wales as he'd promised he would.

"When was the last time you saw your brother?" The girl frowned. Days hadn't much relevance in her life, they followed one another in an uneventful pattern.

"On Sean's birthday," she decided. "He was here then."

"What date was that?"

"Last month. The fifteenth." That settled it. Crispin Sinclair glanced at his watch. He'd have to hurry if he were to get a decent lunch before returning.

"Look, I think I will leave a message after all . . . time's getting on. Please tell your mother I was asking after Evan. And if he does come, would you ask him to call." He gave her his card. "He can leave a message at that number any time." A thought occurred. "Has anyone—any of Evan's other friends been here recently?" She wasn't as stupid as he'd first thought.

"You're from the police, aren't you?"

"What makes you say that? I'm not, as a matter of fact—"

"Is he in trouble?" she persisted.

"No, of course not. I wanted to see him about his new house, actually. I can get building materials at trade discount. Evan was really keen when I told him and I wouldn't want him to miss out." It sounded a reasonable excuse to him but whether the girl believed it was another matter.

"I'll tell Mam you've been." She wanted rid of him. A man in smart clothes with a posh accent was outside the norm, not to be trusted. "She might be a long time because of the buses."

"Yes, of course. Thank you for the tea." She was already in the passage, pulling her cardigan round her before opening the door.

"I'm sorry I missed your brother."

"If Evan's back, he'll be at his house," she repeated. "He and Mam have fixed a date for her visit and I know he wanted to get it finished before then." Crispin decided to give Evan Jones a piece of his mind if that was the reason. Nothing but a wild-goose chase, coming here.

"I'd like to catch up with him before his next trip. Maybe I'll drop by his place. Holt's Farm Cottages, wasn't that it? Down a mile and a half of unmade lane, according to your brother."

The girl looked at him obliquely. "I don't know about the lane; I've not visited it yet."

Careful, he thought. A stranger going to all that trouble? In this street, men in suits probably meant debt-collectors from Carmarthen or Swansea. He paused on the step. "I'm often travelling on the M4," he shouted, above the rain. "Your brother's house isn't much of a detour." But she wasn't interested in that either; she'd already shut the front door.

In Heathrow, the final call for the missing British Airways passenger to Sydney echoed over the Tannoy: "Mr Ray Vincent, proceed to Gate 31 *immediately* for embarkation." The disembodied voice had all the charm of an angry nanny.

He approached Customs unhurriedly and waited until his bag had disappeared into the maw of the X-ray machine before stepping through the scanner. When the buzzer sounded, he automatically took his cigar case out of a breast pocket and handed it over. The Customs man glanced inside before returning it.

At the departure gate, the ground hostess hissed angrily as she saw the missing passenger unzip his overnight bag in response to the officer's request. A gaudily coloured box with gift paper and label lay on top of some clothes.

"I didn't bother to wrap it, I thought you might want to see inside," the passenger said diffidently.

"Quite right, sir. 'To Wayne on his eighth birthday, love from Uncle Ray'—I see." In the cardboard box, dark grey pieces of moulded fibreglass lay in a plastic tray ready for easy assembly. The Customs man looked at the sheet of instructions. "These get more realistic every day, don't they?"

"They do indeed."

"No bullets?"

"No." Ray Vincent smiled. "They make me nervous . . . besides, it's amazing how easily kids can damage themselves, even with toys." The officer shuffled the lid back on and invited the passenger to close up his bag.

"How right you are. Have a pleasant trip."

"Thank you."

Ray Vincent followed the ground hostess's angry back up the aircraft steps. As a design, the weapon was precision-made, Swiss perfection with the few remaining metal parts carefully disposed of within his bag. He'd be glad when the Swiss solved the problem of the bullets though, being a non-smoker.

He fastened his seat-belt and closed his eyes, willing himself to forget. Adele hadn't believed his excuses. "Why now, why today? It's not that long since you told me you wouldn't have to go back East. You never said a word last week when I bought two tickets for the barbecue."

"I didn't know last week, it only cropped up this morning." She'd become even more suspicious.

"When did they call? You said a phone call from New York—"

"At the office. First thing this morning. You can ask Janice if you don't believe me." He cursed himself for admitting too much; there'd been too many slip-ups, he couldn't afford any more.

They hadn't spoken during the drive to Heathrow. Adele slid into the driving seat without offering to kiss him goodbye. "You'll phone? As soon as you know when you're coming back?"

"As soon as the deal's signed, promise. It shouldn't take long, the conveyancing side is all tied up—" But he needn't have bothered because she ignored it.

"I suppose you want me to keep the P-O-N-Y a secret until you return."

"What, and ruin Amy's birthday! Lord, no . . ." He'd bent to hug his plump little daughter who wrinkled her nose as she always did.

"You smell nice, Daddy." Adele immediately contradicted her.

"If you want my opinion, you use too much. It's very strong, Ray." He'd tried to smile. He'd stood in the shower until the water ran cold but he hadn't been able to wash away the memory, not this time, of the hot smell of blood.

"Would you like me to bring you more opals? To match the necklace?"

"I thought you said you'd only be away a couple of days? You'd have to go back to the mine to do that. Will you be away that long?"

The Tannoy calling his name had interrupted and he tried not to sound relieved. "Listen love, must go. Take care—" But Adele was already pulling away from the kerb. He heard Amy wail, "You promised we could wave Daddy's plane goodbye, you promised!"

Sugary music stopped, another nanny told him the flight time and altitude and the vast machine hurtled down the runway. Ray Vincent switched off his reading light and pulled down the blind. A steward was making his way through the cabin with the inevitable champagne cocktails.

He and Zee had made a mistake, using Jones. The organization didn't tolerate mistakes. They'd sent Parker to help him obliterate that mistake . . . the memory of what had happened made Vincent grip the arms convulsively. Parker had actually enjoyed doing it. *He'd* wanted to be quick but Parker insisted on doing it his way. . .

The steward was offering him a drink; Vincent shook his head, breathing hard to regain control. Easy . . . easy. He had the name, he knew where to find her, all he had to do was finish the job, his way. Then it would be over—please God let this be the last time!

"That's Gary, all right." The friendly woman serving in the ice-cream parlour nodded at the photo in recognition. "Taken in England, was it?" Mavis Bignell was delighted.

"Yes, a few years ago. Gary is Ben's father. How marvellous you remembering them. Have you seen them recently?"

"Ben, that's his kid's name, is it?" The woman topped the two knickerbocker glories with dollops of cream. Watching her, Mr Pringle began to feel queasy. Mavis searched through the pile of photos for one of Ben, but when she showed her the friendly woman shook her head.

"Sorry, love. It's nice and clear, you can see what he looks like all right, but I don't remember the kiddie at all. It's not likely I would have met him, is it? Gary used to be a truck driver. They don't allow them to carry passengers."

"Ben sent his grandma a postcard from Bathurst." Mavis found it in her bag. "Look, he's marked this place."

"Oh, yeah . . . We sell those. Maybe Gary bought it here? Or at the post office?"

"Read the message," Mavis urged. "Ben says he had an ice-cream." The woman reached for her spectacles. She wasn't as young as Mr Pringle first thought; blonde hair had been dulled by middle-age and constant exposure to the sun emphasized the wrinkles as it did for so many women out here.

"Did the kiddie write this?" she asked.

"Yes," replied Mavis. "His grandma, my friend Mrs Hardie I was telling you about, she got it from him a few months ago."

"Well, I haven't seen Gary for a long time." The woman broke off to attend to another customer. "Yes? What'll it be?"

"Coke," said Charlie.

"I told you it wouldn't be difficult," Mrs Bignell whispered conspiratorially. "Ben must've come here with Gary. Maybe Gary kept him out of sight? Because of the rules about passengers?"

"Possibly. I shouldn't get too excited. We don't want to arouse false hopes in Mrs Hardie."

Mr Pringle plunged the long spoon in as far as the bright green jelly. He'd leave the cherry till last like he always did.

"Must be all of six months since Gary was here." The woman had returned. "He'd been laid off, poor fella. He was hoping to find work up country." She sighed. "It's not easy nowadays. Too much competition. And Gary had stayed in England too long, he'd lost his contacts."

"It was his wife who was the problem," said Mrs Bignell. "Linda. Did he tell you about her?"

The woman behind the counter didn't reply. Instead she said, "Gary always told me he was willin' to turn his hand to anythin'."

"Perhaps he went on a sheep station?" Mr Pringle's knowledge of Australia was sketchy and the woman laughed in a kindly way.

"You need an awful lot of skill to handle sheep, it's not somethin' you can pick up easily. No, I reckon Gary's in the Northern Territories. Maybe Katherine. Or Alice. They're always advertising for workers up in there, 'cause it's too bloody hot. People can't stick it for long."

Mavis and Mr Pringle had a brief discussion. They would send another postcard to Mrs Hardie, Mavis decided, and Mr Pringle dissuaded her from writing "Hot on the trail!"

"It's extremely unlikely we will find the boy. He's of school age. His father must have arranged that he live somewhere permanent in order to attend one. Gary could hardly take the child along when looking for work."

"And Gary was broke." The woman behind the counter was sad. "He was down to his last few dollars. He was hitchin', which ain't the best way to travel in this country."

"Perhaps we should leave a little something?" Mavis enquired delicately. The friendly lady suddenly went pink.

"No need," she insisted. "If Gary turns up again, he'll be looked after." And Mr Pringle had to kick Mavis on the shin to stop her asking any more questions.

It wasn't going to work, Mrs Hardie admitted it to herself, not ever. She was certain of it now. The house hadn't been cleaned, not by her standards. Immobile on the sofa, the cast on her leg anchoring her to the downstairs back room, she gazed at polish smears, dull brass and dust. Linda had attempted to clean. On the mirror above the fireplace there were streaky marks and the distinct imprint of her fingers where she'd held it steady. She'd used one of those aerosol things. They made everything worse in Mrs Hardie's opinion.

It hadn't taken long for her to drop back into her old habits, either. Mrs Hardie's mouth twitched. The table lamp was on, she could see the clock. Two a.m. and her daughter still wasn't in. When she did return, she'd probably be drunk. Mrs Hardie scolded herself vigorously for not accepting the welfare lady's advice. Fancy letting Linda talk her out of it—all that nonsense about needing a garden for Ben to play in—as if Gary would give the boy up even if Mavis and her friend did manage to find him.

Oddly enough, the garden was the one thing Linda had tackled. Through the window Mrs Hardie could make out the rockery against the solid darkness of the trim lawn.

In the warden flats, you didn't have to worry about gardening; all that was taken care of. As soon as the home help came tomorrow and after Linda had gone to work, Mrs Hardie would ask her to make that phone call. To the welfare lady. Surely *she* wouldn't have reallocated the vacant flat already?

It was very late but Crispin Sinclair decided to break his journey after all. Better that and have all the answers ready for the inevitable inquisition tomorrow morning.

His irritability increased as he bumped down the track—it wasn't doing his suspension any good at all—that Jones could be so stupid as to stay where he could be found! The chap didn't deserve any help.

The two cottages were in darkness, which was a blow. Crispin banged on each front door in turn then, deciding he would leave a note because Jones was obviously out boozing somewhere, searched for a stick to push the Filofax page through the letter-box. Passing the back door, he tried the handle and found it wasn't locked.

The air-traffic controller drove the last few yards much more carefully. He travelled the lane often and knew the potholes. There was a movement ahead—someone was leaving the house next door. Had Jones finally returned? It was dark, he didn't recognize the silhouette.

The controller turned into his own parking space and switched off the ignition. Odd, the stranger hadn't moved. He still leaned against the open door front, almost clung to it. The controller could see clearly now that it definitely wasn't Jones.

For a moment or two, he stayed where he was. Silly to be so cautious, no doubt, but these cottages were isolated. Winding down the window he called, "Is Evan back? Have you seen him?" Almost as an afterthought he added, "I've got a bone to pick with him. He must've let some food go bad, the smell's been awful lately." He broke off. Whoever the stranger was, he'd turned away and was vomiting frantically into a patch of grass.

The controller left his car and hurried across. The stranger, whey-faced and shaking, was on his knees. When he looked up there were tears streaming down his face. "Police. . .quick as you can. For God's sake, don't go in there! Close the fucking door!"

Chapter Twelve

The further they were from Sydney, the more Mr Pringle's courage returned. He questioned Mrs Bignell gently, he didn't want to rekindle their quarrel, but he had to know how much she'd told Evan.

"I said we were hoping to find Ben."

"Did you describe our route in detail?"

"I don't think so . . ." She answered slowly. "I said we were sharing a coach with the FONEs—we had a laugh about that. Why d'you ask? You're not still worried about that powder, whatever it was?"

"Yes, I am. Whoever it belongs to is bound to come for it." Mavis looked at the miles of empty road ahead and the bare landscape on either side.

"He'll be a bit conspicuous if he does . . . all the same, there aren't many police about, either. Tell you what, dear, I promise not to pick up any more strange men. Even if a gorgeous bit of crumpet tries to chat me up, I shan't even listen. Now I can't say fairer than that, can I?" He hadn't the heart to insist the matter was serious.

They arrived at their destination, Coonabarabran, and the El Paso Motel. As their coach turned into the car-park, Mavis said approvingly, "Very Spanish."

The FONEs liked it, too. A familiar landscape of trees and green hills had been left far behind. Once beyond the Great Dividing Range, they'd begun to appreciate how vast and hostile this land was; mile upon mile of meagre vegetation following years of drought. Coming from England it had to be experienced to be understood. Here they were back in civilization where there were hot showers and comfortable beds.

The motel was single-storey with a steep red-tiled roof and deep white arches concealing the reception buildings. On either side, conifers cast dark shadows. "They've got a proper restaurant, it says so on the sign. D'you think there'll be a band?"

"Goodness, I doubt it!"

Protheroe was already marshalling his troops. Tonight, the FONEs were scheduled to meet members of the public. As Friends they were about to preach on the benefits of nuclear disposal and "sound out local opinion", as Protheroe put it. Mr Pringle thought it prudent if he and Mavis distanced themselves.

"You never know, they might have a band . . ." Mrs Bignell sounded wistful. She waited as Charlie and Len unloaded the baggage. Trundling her suitcase, she followed Mr Pringle to where Protheroe was handing out the keys. "Herbert and I used to go to the Palais regularly, on Latin-American nights."

It wasn't often that the late Mr Bignell was referred to and Mr Pringle listened attentively. "If Herbert hadn't needed a partner for the *pasa doble* competition, we might never have got together," she sighed; "and when he turned up that evening, in white tie and tails, that was it. I'd never seen anyone dressed like Fred Astaire before. I only found out afterwards they belonged to his uncle who was a mason. Herbert was a good dancer, though," she said loyally. "We did get as far as the final eight." Mr Pringle was silent for a moment, in tribute.

"I'm afraid I don't dance."

"No, I know." For Mavis, this was no consolation. "Still, there's one or two FONEs come without their wives," she said, brightening, "and they're not dangerous, so if there is a band, I think I might wear my red lace."

Anthony Pelham-Walker's confident air had disappeared. Alone, apart from Macillvenny, in a vast burnt-out wilderness, he'd no one to blame but himself; he longed, though, for the familiar protection of the department. Kev tried to interest him in the sights.

"See those white parakeets? Typical they are . . ." Pelham-Walker yearned for a humble sparrow. "We'll be drivin' past the Warrumbungles tomorrow," Kev went on. "Thirteen million years ago they were formed, after a huge volcanic explosion."

What were Greenwich or Whitehall compared to that? The sight of ordinary houses and streets in a town was suddenly as reassuring as a lifebelt to a drowning man.

Kev booked rooms at the Country Comfort Motel. Pelham-Walker let him take charge. He watched apathetically as Kev phoned first Charlie, then the office in Macquarie Street. With nothing to interest him, Anthony Pelham-Walker found his thoughts drifting homeward towards Fiona: what would she get up to while he was away?

Unpleasant possibilities flooded his tired brain—he must get back at once! What on earth was he thinking of, wandering aimlessly round this benighted country? Kev's voice broke through his confusion: "Give me that bit again?" Anthony Pelham-Walker felt depressed. He no longer wanted to hear of any developments, he wanted to go home.

"That's great," said Kev. "Send the bloke a message from me. Tell him I think he deserves a medal. Anything else?" He frowned. "Nothing more . . . ?" He swivelled round. "What's your fella's name again?"

"Sinclair. Crispin Sinclair."

"Yeah . . . anything come in from Sinclair?" He replaced the receiver, obviously displeased. "What's Sinclair think he's doing? He's had enough time."

Anthony Pelham-Walker forced himself to consider the return journey to Wales. "We should hear something soon," he agreed, "unless they're resurfacing the M4. They often do at this time of year." Kev worked out the implication for himself.

"You don't mean Sinclair's gone by car? Why not hire a plane?" Anthony Pelham-Walker tried to bridge the gulf.

"In England . . . in my department . . . no one hires an aircraft without special permission from the Minister, which could take months, and in Sinclair's grade, wouldn't be granted for any reason whatsoever. It'll be difficult justifying a journey to Carmarthen at 31.3 pence per mile as it is."

"But Pelham . . . we're all of us trying to break up a drug racket."

"We're trying equally hard at our end, believe me, Macillvenny. Any criticism—"

"At 31.3 pence per mile!"

"If we can't prove we're cost-effective, we risk being wound up altogether."

"You can't be serious! My God Pelham, that's terrible." Kev was stunned by the parsimony. "How in hell are you supposed to catch villains under those conditions?"

"I honestly don't know," Pelham-Walker said wearily. "Fortunately that is seldom my concern."

"Cheer up. We may have had a bit of luck. One of your Customs officers was on the ball. A passenger for Sydney turned up at Heathrow with one of those 9mm semi-automatic Heckler & Koch plastic pistols. Had it in pieces like an assembly toy but your bloke spotted it. He knew the sort of gun that *should* have been in the cardboard box because his kid's got a similar one. When he picked it up, it felt too heavy, that's what made him look closely. No identification, all carefully removed. Smart of the officer to think of checking that. Fortunately, Heathrow made the decision not to intercept but to send us a signal. They've circulated those departments who might be concerned, including ours of course. Nice to have some co-operation from the mother country once in a while." The sarcasm was ignored.

"Is the passenger known to you?"

"They're still checking him out," Kev replied. "He's a businessman who visits Sydney occasionally, name of Vincent. Says in his passport he's an estate agent—which he's not. You don't need that sort of pistol in the property business.

"Your bloke didn't spot any ammunition but maybe Vincent's got training bullets concealed someplace."

"What are those?"

"If he's a pro, and with a gun like that what else could he be, he needs to practise."

They were into realms that Anthony Pelham-Walker had only read about, and not in interdepartmental memos. He was very frightened indeed. "Do you think he might be carrying real bullets as well?" he asked tremulously.

"We'll find out when he gets here," Kev grinned. He looked at his watch. "Take-off was o-nine-thirty British Summer Time . . . Twenty-two hour flight—he should get here early tomorrow. Our blokes will be waiting. By then, we should have off the computer everything there is to know about Ray Vincent."

"According to Lenny," said Mavis, "tomorrow morning we're going to see the koala. It lives in a national park not far away from here." Despite the lack of a band, the evening hadn't been a disappointment. First there was the discovery that Mrs Bignell's favourite drink, port, was not only available, it was manufactured in quantity in Australia. After that, with so many varieties to sample, the El Paso restaurant had taken on a roseate glow.

For Mr Pringle, the sight of his fellow countrymen setting forth on their mission had provided a memory to treasure. Protheroe's instruction had been to "blend in" with the local population and the scientists had done their best. Trousers had been abandoned but not brown socks and buckled sandals. Shorts revealed the forced rhubarb pallor of British knees. Heads were topped with inappropriate Australian hats and, worst of all, Protheroe sported a T-shirt with a saucy emu on the chest.

As they trooped outside he called, "Remember, our hosts this evening are the Lions of Coonabarabran," and they sallied forth; Daniels, every one.

Lenny and Pete watched incredulously. "Are they in disguise?"

"Yeah," said Pete, "they're pretendin' to be Kiwis."

"You know," said Mavis as they went back to their room, "I'm getting a bit fed up with those FONEs, they're giving the British a bad name. I wish we'd decided to travel independently; we could look for Ben properly on our own." Mr Pringle had indulged in sufficient port to make him reckless.

"There's nothing to stop us hiring a car. We could catch up with the coaches later on. Pete and Lenny are travelling in easy stages." Mavis hugged him, eyes shining.

"We can talk to the ice-cream lady again? You know the sort of questions to ask. There wasn't nearly enough time this morning." Already Mr Pringle was regretting his gesture.

"It's a long way back to Bathurst."

"Yes, but the roads are so much quieter out here. And I'm sure that woman knew Gary."

"She may not be willing to tell us," he warned.

"Oh, you'll manage." Mavis squeezed his arm. "It's amazing how you can coax people when you want. Come on, let's find out about hire-cars." Mr Pringle remained where he was.

"Mavis, there is a serious problem if we do go it alone."

"You mean—because of the powder?" He nodded.

"At least Protheroe and his lunatics give us a degree of protection. Alone with me, your life could be in danger."

He looked so grave, Mavis shivered. "You're not just trying to frighten me?"

"I've concealed my fears until now for the sake of our holiday, but the risk is there. In my opinion, it's a serious one." She considered for a moment or two.

"Well, if I went back without doing my best, I'd never forgive myself." Mr Pringle accepted this with a sinking heart.

"I think we should try and rejoin the coach during their stay at Ayers Rock. That gives us nearly three days for our search."

"Oh, yes, I don't want to miss that. They said in *Reader's Digest* it was the eighth wonder of the world."

"Ah," he murmured, "they so often do."

Kev picked up the receiver: "Yes?"

"It's me," said Charlie. "Change of plan this end. The seed packet's going back to Bathurst to look for that kid she was talking about. Pete's fixing up a hire-car deal for the two of 'em right this minute. They're leaving early tomorrow."

"Stick with her," Kev ordered. "Offer to drive if you can. We'll follow."

"Right." Kev replaced the receiver.

"We're heading back, Pelham," he said. "This could be interesting."

"Oh yes?" Another long day on the road . . . with another Chinese take-away at the end of it? Why was it at the opposite ends of the earth the food was always the same?

He was leaving to return to his own room when he had a sudden thought. "Missionaries?"

"Pardon?" asked Kev.

"You said, the house in Byers Street was occupied by missionaries."

"They're genuine. We checked them out."

"But wasn't there a priest involved when that chap was hanged in Penang?"

"My word, Pelham, so there was!" Kev stared. "Better watch out. Could be you got a talent for this type of work after all."

In the El Paso Motel, Mr Pringle examined Ben's last postcard again. He looked at the message. What had the friendly woman said? "Did the kid write this?"

Had she really no idea where Gary had hidden the child? Their relationship was, Mr Pringle guessed, a close one. Was she protecting a lover who'd kidnapped his only son?

He added the postcard to the photographs of Ben. Top of the pile was the most recent. He could understand why Mrs Protheroe had suggested rickets. The boy had the same fragile bones as his grandmother and the thin legs were slightly bowed. The blue eyes were compelling, such an intense colour, the whites reflected it.

Perhaps the film had had a blue tint? Mr Pringle's snaps often turned out a funny colour. He yawned and stretched. "Ready for bed?"

"Yes, I am." Mavis fixed him with a stern gaze. "And we'll save our strength tonight if you don't mind."

After his recent exertions, he was only too glad to comply.

In England it was half-past ten in the morning. The home help let herself back in. "How d'you get on?" asked Mrs Hardie eagerly.

"The welfare lady said she can't promise you another flat but she will come round and talk to you about it. I told her where she could find the key and when you'd be on your own; she said to say she quite understood. She'll be round by the end of the week."

The girl glanced at the clock. "If I get a move on, I can do the bathroom as well as the kitchen before I go."

She disappeared and Mrs Hardie limped across to the mantelpiece. None of the ornaments had been done. The girl hadn't been trained; all she did was flip a duster and leave it at that. The sooner

Mrs Hardie had a place of her own where she could do the cleaning properly, the better. As she hobbled back to the sofa, the girl called from the kitchen, "You're nearly out of washing-up liquid, did you know?"

Chapter Thirteen

"They heckled Kenneth!" Jean Protheroe was tearfully angry. "He'd set aside time for questions but they wouldn't even let him finish his speech!"

"How rude!" said Mavis.

"Dear me," murmured Mr Pringle. He tried to appear sympathetic as he continued to load their luggage plus tents and sleeping-bags into the hire-car.

"Kenneth's got a migraine this morning as well as asthma. It's the strain, you know. He kept telling them about the benefits but they refused to listen."

"What—benefits?" Mr Pringle paused, mystified.

"Becoming world leader in the disposal of nuclear waste, of course," Mrs Protheroe replied, tartly. "Australia could be ahead of the Japanese for once if only they'd listen."

"But isn't the government here against—" Mr Pringle began, then winced as Mrs Bignell stepped on his foot.

"The Australians have elected a government that's hand in glove with big business, so they're bound to understand the benefits." Mrs Protheroe spoke with conviction. "Which is why it was so surprising when one of the natives began shouting abuse."

Seeing his expression, Mavis explained, "I think Jean means one of the black ones don't you, Jean? An Aboriginal native."

"Yes. I'd no idea they let them out of their compounds. I thought they stayed in designated areas, going walkabout whenever their goats had eaten all the pasture . . ."

Jean Protheroe had a clear bell-like tone and Mr Pringle glanced round nervously to ensure neither Lenny nor Pete was within earshot.

"We didn't imagine for a moment *they*'d be invited to the meeting, to make trouble for Kenneth."

"I think it's the bedouins who have goats, Jean, not the Aborigines." Mavis looked at Mr Pringle for confirmation. He threw discretion to the winds.

"Surely the whole purpose of your visit was to arrange for the disposal of nuclear waste beneath Aborigine homelands? Under those circumstances are they not entitled to ask questions, and protest?"

Jean Protheroe's expression changed; this was one of those whingeing lefties the Prime Minister was always warning about! "I don't think you've understood, Mr Pringle. Kenneth and his colleagues have travelled all this way to explain to a backward people how their empty deserts can be made profitable. What's more," she warmed to her theme, "FONE are prepared to retrain any natives who live on those sites to handle the waste under a special YTS scheme. They'll be able to earn their living whilst remaining in their compounds. The Australian government are bound to see the advantages and the Japanese are queueing up to be the first to bury their plutonium. But we need support to make these simple people understand—and now you're deserting us." She made it sound like a crime.

"Only for two days," Mavis protested.

Mr Pringle asked mildly, "If the natives become radioactive, will they still be allowed to go walkabout?" Fortunately Charlie arrived in the nick of time.

"You folks ready to leave?" He turned to Mrs Protheroe. "We'll be meeting you again at Ayers Rock."

"Possibly not," she said darkly. "Kenneth may decide to cancel the tour altogether." She strode away and Charlie opened the passenger door for Mavis.

"Would you like me to drive?" he asked politely.

"Oh, would you, dear? It would be easier for us if you did. How kind of Pete and Lenny to spare you."

"We need a few things for the coach. Pete wants me to pick 'em up in Bathurst."

In such a small town, thought Mr Pringle, how odd? He sat in the back and wondered about Charlie. He hadn't been at Kingsford Smith when they'd arrived but then neither had the cook, Sheri. Of course they hadn't, they weren't needed that day, either of them; there was no need to worry. Charlie was an employee of Wallaby Tours not part of a drug syndicate; he'd be a useful ally if anything occurred, young and strong. Ought Mr Pringle to explain there could be a problem? Should he, in fact, take Charlie into his confidence?

Mavis was chattering away telling him of their search. Mr Pringle decided to remain silent. She'd assured him again last night that Evan knew nothing other than that they were travelling with the FONEs. Surely now they'd departed from that itinerary, he and Mavis would be even more secure?

A cold wind blew down the Carmarthen street, whipping up discarded greasy wrappings from outside the chippy. The middle-aged woman holding the door open a crack spoke quickly out of chilly nervousness, "Yes, what d'you want?"

The young WPC said gently, "Mrs Jones? Can we come in, love? It's. . .personal." The woman, dark-haired, blue-eyed with a tired tense face, sensed something even colder than the wind in the way one of them couldn't meet her gaze.

"Not all of you." She wanted to delay whatever it was as long as possible. "There's too many with only me and Lesley here."

The CID man who'd been avoiding her suddenly looked up; she saw the pity in his eyes. "We haven't done anything wrong," she whispered. Her heart was thumping as the policewoman spoke again.

"No, it's nothing like that. It's about Evan, love."

Crispin Sinclair was in his flat, suspended from duty until the results of police enquiries were known. He couldn't stop shivering. He knew he wouldn't sleep despite the pills his lover had given him. "The department kept insisting it was *my* responsibility," he repeated; and his lover replied automatically, "Yes, you said. Bloody nerve."

"They claimed I'd let the fool walk into a trap—I kept telling him to go to Wales—"

"Yes, I know."

"They said I should have handed him over to the police straight away—"

"Well you should. We both know that."

"Don't you start!" The youth looked wounded.

"All I meant was, if it hadn't been for Batman, you would've gone to them, wouldn't you? The police?" There was a pause. "Well, wouldn't you?"

"Oh, shut up!" Crispin shivered so violently this time his lover became alarmed.

"I'll get you some cocoa . . . How about a hot-water bottle, that might help?" From the kitchen, he called out, "Here . . . have you replied to that telex yet? The one Batman sent from Sydney?"

"Shut up about the blasted telex. What the department really wants is for me to resign!" The youth stood in the doorway, cocoa tin in hand.

"Yes, you said. Poor old bear. What a bloody nerve!" Without warning, tears began coursing down Crispin's face.

"It was so awful! They'd bashed him to pulp with that hammer—blood and brains everywhere!" His lover's gorge began to rise.

"Oh, for Chrissake, heart!" It was no use, he'd always been sensitive; he dropped the tin and dashed to the bathroom.

The British Airways flight taxied to a halt at Kingsford Smith and passengers began to disembark. Scrutinizing them from the arrival building were two immigration officials. Inside, waiting on the concourse, were airport security guards and, in an unmarked car outside, the police.

At Immigration desks, each official knew the name: Ray Vincent was to be allowed through as far as the concourse to see whether anyone contacted him, before being taken in for questioning.

From their vantage point, the officials watched the crowd gather in the arrival hall below. Two 747s had arrived simultaneously which meant there were several hundred milling about.

Radio contact between the tower and the BA flight had worked perfectly. The purser indicated unobtrusively as Ray Vincent descended the steps, a member of the ground staff followed the passenger into the arrival hall and now, as the officials watched from the viewing gallery, brushed past casually as Vincent joined the waiting crowd.

"That must be him. On the left—light-coloured mac, carrying a navy overnight bag!"

"Got him." The second man moved to a wall phone and passed the information through to Passport Control.

Below, passengers stood patiently behind white lines and approached Immigration singly or in pairs when beckoned to do so. Gradually, the mass of bodies shuffled forward. Not until Ray Vincent was at the front did the two watching him make a move.

As he stepped up to a desk and they heard their colleague say "Good morning, Mr Vincent," they slipped past screens and took up position on either side of the concourse, ready to identify him to the guards. There were now four people to watch every move Ray Vincent made.

The first guard spoke into his radio: "Suspect has arrived at Passport Control. Coming through any minute now."

"Check."

By the carousel, the crowd waiting for their luggage was three to four deep. The two guards moved closer in.

"Business or pleasure, sir?"

"A bit of both, I hope." Ray Vincent's entry document was in order. The officer stamped his passport and returned it. "Enjoy your visit. Your luggage will be arriving shortly."

"Many thanks." Vincent gave an easy smile but instead of moving forward, went towards the transit desk, increasing his speed to a brisk trot. He pushed his way to the front, cash in hand. "Excuse me . . . sorry. Look, any chance of the next flight to Brisbane? My wife's terribly sick." The accent was Australian and the clerk scarcely looked up as he referred to his screen.

"Sorry to hear that. Will club class suit?"

"Fine, thanks. The name's Walsh, John Walsh." Ray Vincent was already peeling dollars off the roll. "Keep the change—give it to charity."

"Thank you, sir." The clerk called after him, "Last call was five minutes ago, I'll tell them you're on your way—TAA 464, Gate 15, Mr Walsh!" People waited sympathetically as the clerk confirmed it over his mike to ground control.

It took nearly four minutes for the Immigration official to get from his desk to a guard, another two minutes for them to reach the transit desk and a further minute to establish what had happened. By then, the aircraft containing "John Walsh" was taxiing toward the main runway.

The first officer had to complete his take-off checks before he could attend to the signal from the tower and pass it to the chief steward. He and the purser checked the seating plan but Ray Vincent was no longer in club class, he was recovering his nerve in one of the tourist washrooms.

Something had gone badly wrong! He'd planned every move—it had been damn tight because the BA flight had been behind schedule, but he'd made it, thank God! But why had those guards been on the look out? He was hyped up, he always was on a job, and when the man brushed past he knew the reason instinctively. Experience got him through the rest of it—but why?

Mirrors reflected the fleshy face, the gut that was beginning to be noticeable. Ray Vincent gripped the wash-basin. Why were they looking for him? They couldn't possibly connect him with Jones. What the hell had gone wrong? The infinite mirrored reflections were taut with fear.

After five minutes, he'd got his breathing under control. There was probably some damn-fool explanation. He'd get on with what he had to do; there wasn't time to worry about anything else.

He folded his poplin mac in a tight small roll, unzipped his bag and began. He exchanged his British passport for an American one concealed in the stiffening at the bottom, packed the cardboard box in its gift paper, flushing away the original label and replacing it with one that read "To Philip from Uncle Greg".

He sprayed his fair hair grey, combed it flat and parted it on the opposite side.

Changing his shirt and tie for a T-shirt, he put on a seersucker jacket bought in San Francisco. Finally, he stuck a scrap of bloodstained lint and plaster to his jaw.

When cabin staff banged on the door and told him they were approaching Brisbane, Ray Vincent limped to an empty seat at the back of the rear cabin.

He was among the first tourist passengers down the steps and across the tarmac, putting on blue-tinted glasses against the glare of the Brisbane sun. The slight limp and hunched shoulders didn't prevent him keeping up with the crowd.

The TAA terminal was cool and airy with rows of grey seating and plants hanging from the high-tech rafters. The elderly American limped with the rest past more security guards who were scrutinizing them again. He hadn't imagined it, they were looking for him! Ray Vincent kept an even pace, instinct again, but his heart beat painfully.

It was an internal flight, there were no formalities. He was free to walk outside and join a bus queue.

He waited until all those in the line for taxis had been driven away. When the next vacant cab drew up, the "American" appeared to change his mind, hailed it and disappeared.

The driver chattered occasionally. His passenger listened, looking to right and left as though a stranger in the elegant city. His blue glasses had thick lenses; they added years to his age as did his hesitant speech. Ray Vincent peered uncertainly at the address in his diary. "Canberra Hotel?"

"Sure. It's in Ann Street. Not smart, but nice and central."

"Good . . . Don't find walking that easy . . ."

The Canberra was a warren of three hundred cramped, old-fashioned rooms. When, an hour later, Ray Vincent walked through reception a second time, none of the desk clerks paid attention.

He was an anonymous businessman now, sufficiently tanned to pass for an Australian, in a short-sleeved shirt and tie. The cardboard box was inside a salesman's zip-case with a company logo across one corner: Leigh Plastics. Blue-tinted glasses had been exchanged for bifocals with thick tortoise-shell frames, and the shaving cut had vanished.

He still had difficulty controlling his breathing—he was too old for the job. Out of practice. He'd ask to see them in New York, do a deal. Pull out. Did anyone ever get to retire? Would they allow him to? Careful planning had got him this far but could he keep it up?

Even though he was sure he wasn't being followed, Ray Vincent automatically doubled back twice on the short walk, coming out at the back of the coach station before dodging the traffic on North Quay and crossing the bridge. He bought a paper from a news-stand. On a bench overlooking the river Zee waited for him.

"Look, something's gone wrong."

"They are angry in New York," Zee said. "Very angry." The blood pumped even faster. Zee slid his evening paper across the seat between them. It was open at the foreign news page. "Jones has been found."

"So?" Vincent was aggressive. "We knew he would be. There's nothing there—" He stabbed the brief paragraph "—to connect him with *us*."

Zee then asked, "So why d'you insist something is wrong? Here . . ." A small plastic box slid across under cover of the paper. Ray Vincent opened the lid without looking at it and ran a finger over the contents to reassure himself. Could he risk telling Zee about the security guards waiting at Kingsford Smith? If New York really was angry . . . The Brisbane sun no longer felt warm.

"They say you and Parker went crazy."

"Listen, don't blame me—that maniac actually enjoys what he's doing!" Pent up fear made Vincent garrulous. "You weren't there—when he'd got hold of that hammer, the saliva was oozing out!"

"It was your operation. All identification should have been removed and the body hidden where it couldn't be found." Vincent didn't speak. Zee watched him check the yellow label on the box. "Six dozen 88-grain, hollow-point configuration, as you requested," he said automatically. He never raised his voice even though it could scarcely be heard above the traffic on North Quay.

Vincent's hand closed over the cold bullets. Of course he and Parker should have obliterated all traces! He'd slipped up. Parker had only been sent in because he'd failed originally to get the information out of Jones. Another mistake—and New York didn't permit those. The hard edge of the plastic box bit into his palm.

"This is their itinerary." Zee pulled out a copy of the FONEs' travel plan, stained and covered with cigarette ash, obviously retrieved from a waste bin. He passed it across, aware as always of the other's Western smell.

Ray Vincent said dully, "What's going to happen?" Zee immediately distanced himself.

"I leave here tonight for good."

"Where are you. . . ?" But Vincent bit back the question. Zee wouldn't tell him, it was against the rules. Zee stood, tucking the paper neatly under his arm.

"According to the English newspapers, Jones was found by a contact from the British Home Office." He watched as the implication sank home.

"Oh, Christ!" Vincent stared at Zee, fear making his stomach lurch and his voice hoarse. The double-crossing Welsh bastard! That was why they'd been on the look-out. "I haven't got a chance!"

Zee asked simply, "You have what you need?" Vincent nodded dumbly. "New York also said . . ." He hesitated.

"What?"

"Remember your daughter, Amy." Zee walked away across the bridge and Ray Vincent watched him go.

They were alone but Mrs Hardie and the welfare lady talked quietly, like conspirators.

"It's not the same flat, that one's gone. This is on the corner of the block. It's nice but it doesn't get quite as much sun. You'll have to give me a definite yes as soon as you can. D'you want time to think it over?"

Mrs Hardie shook her head vehemently. "I should have said yes last time."

The welfare lady was full of regret. "It hardly ever works . . . a married daughter returns home, starts sharing a kitchen . . . there's bound to be friction. I had hoped you'd be nicely settled by now. Is your leg healing all right?"

"Yes . . ." Mrs Hardie looked at her fearfully. "There's nothing wrong, I start therapy next week."

"Good. Now, what about your daughter, have you told her?"

"No, and don't you say anything, neither."

"But—the tenancy here can't be passed on, you know. This is a three-bed unit; Linda wouldn't qualify."

"I'll tell her once it's definite. She interfered last time. I don't want to miss my chance again."

"We'll wait until the paperwork's complete. It'll take about three weeks. They always redecorate, too, so it's nice and clean. I know how fussy you can be." She laughed again, not unkindly because this was one of the few aspects of her job that gave pleasure: another unwanted old person about to be rehoused satisfactorily.

"The previous tenant left a cooker, a fridge and so forth. Why not give yours to Linda? It might soften the blow when you break the news."

"Yes, all right." Mrs Hardie remembered the angry scenes last time. "I want to do what I can." She was relaxing by the minute; all she had to do was keep the secret a little bit longer.

"Fine." The welfare lady was anxious to be off. "I'll keep in touch."

Crispin Sinclair lay in bed doped with sleeping pills watching his lover pack. "What you doing that for?"

"Don't be a prat!"

"What?" He tried to focus fuzzy thoughts. "What d'you mean?"

"You saw the news."

"So? The police have told the media, what about it?" The youth spun round.

"I'm getting out because I don't want my head bashed in with a hammer." Crispin stared at him. "Think about it!" the youth shouted. "Work it out for yourself. *They*'ve just told everybody that poor Welsh bastard was discovered by 'a representative of the Home Office'."

"They didn't give my name—"

"Everyone in the department knows it was you—that information isn't classified. How long before those friends of his, the ones that killed him, decide you might know something?"

"They wouldn't turn up here!" Crispin Sinclair was open-mouthed. His lover shoved a stack of compact discs on top of his clothes and fastened the suitcase. "Don't be ridiculous!" Crispin struggled out of bed and followed him into the hall. "You can't mean it?" The youth turned, his hand on the Yale lock.

"If I was you, heart, I'd get these changed for something big and heavy. Fix a chain. Tell them downstairs your life's in danger—" He broke off because Crispin was laughing at him. "Suit yourself," he snarled and slammed the door behind him.

Chapter Fourteen

It took all day to return to Bathurst, partly because in Dubbo, where they stopped for tea, Mavis insisted on showing Ben's photo in every café she could find. People were kind, but none remembered seeing the boy. As they resumed their journey she said thoughtfully, "I suppose I could be asking in the wrong sort of place. Lorry drivers don't stop in the middle of towns, do they, because of parking?"

"That's right," replied Charlie.

"Perhaps we should ask at transport cafés instead?"

"Depends what time you plan on gettin' to Bathurst. You given any thought to where you're going to sleep tonight?"

The question sounded innocent enough but much to Mr Pringle's chagrin, by the time they drove into the town Mavis declared she preferred another motel rather than a tent. When he protested she said simply, "Charlie's been telling me about the spiders. Did you know there's one that can give you a fatal bite? A horny funnel red-back, wasn't that what you said it was, dear?" In the driving mirror Charlie's face gave nothing away. Not having read *Reader's Digest*, Mr Pringle couldn't dispute it.

"That spider's only active in this particular area," Mavis said placatingly. "It's safe to use campsites in other places."

Charlie was relieved it had been so easy. Guarding the seed packet inside a motel room was the way he wanted it. He'd think of another excuse tomorrow, depending on where they ended up.

Dropping the pair outside the parlour, he circled the town until he saw Kev's Toyota. Kev was waiting for him. "I've booked three rooms at the hotel across the way. They're going in the middle one. Where are they now?"

"Eating ice-cream and tryin' to find out about that kid. What's the problem?"

"Vincent's on the loose. He dodged them at Sydney and caught a plane to Brisbane, but they didn't pick him up when he landed there."

"Shit! Do we know anything about him yet, like whether there's a connection?" Kev shook his head.

"No, but we're not taking risks even if there is no way he could get to Bathurst today. Stay with them, Charlie. There's bad news from London, too. Jones has been found murdered. Pelham's on the phone now, tryin' to find out all they know about that as well as Vincent. Dammit, someone somewhere must know about him."

The short-sighted American tourist registered as Greg Fischer checked out of the Canberra Hotel in Brisbane less than three hours after he'd registered. A noisy group of sales reps milling around the foyer distracted the cashier's attention. It was only later he noticed the short length of the visit, and that Fischer had paid for a full twenty-four hours.

Despite his limp, Fischer moved quickly down Ann Street to the coach station. His feet tapped an inexorable rhythm on the pavement; Amy, Amy . . . God help anyone who laid a finger on her!

Inside the coach station, he locked himself in a cubicle in the gents'. When Ray Vincent emerged, he wore neat Australian slacks and a sports shirt purchased that afternoon in Leichhardt Street. Some of his other clothes, including his English raincoat, he disposed of in a garbage can together with the remains of the cardboard box and wrapping paper. The 9mm pistol was now reassembled inside the slim salesman's briefcase and the thick tinted glasses had been exchanged for the tortoise-shell rims. He walked out of the back of the coach station and hailed a cab to the airport.

"Yes, sir, can I help you?"

"Judd, passenger for Broken Hill. I telephoned earlier."

"Ah, yes, Mr Judd, I have your reservation. Your flight leaves in half an hour."

Ray Vincent bought an evening paper and a cup of coffee. He badly wanted a drink. Tired taut nerves reawakened aches and pains in his neglected body. He needed a week's hard work-out in a gym—instead he'd got nothing but travel ahead. And at the end of it. . . ? He put that thought firmly out of his mind as he'd trained himself to—if only he could do the same with Amy. He forced himself to read the paper.

Nothing more about Evan Jones, which wasn't surprising. He checked the FONEs' itinerary again. Tonight they were due at Gilgandra, tomorrow, Wilcannia, within driving distance of Broken Hill. There'd be barely half a day before he met up with Mavis Hilda Bignell. Not long but his plan was ready. When it was over, he'd catch the next direct flight home, he wouldn't stop until his daughter was in his arms.

"Ansett announce the departure of their flight AN62 to Broken Hill calling at Bourke . . . ." Ray Vincent swallowed the rest of his coffee.

The friendly lady wasn't behind the counter. Mavis and Mr Pringle consumed banana splits and considered the problem. "I wonder if that new waitress knows Gary was the other lady's boyfriend."

"Go very carefully, Mavis. The other lady might not want the fact generally known."

Mrs Bignell waited until the waitress brought them tea before introducing the topic. "We popped in here yesterday. We were trying to find out about a little boy called Ben. This is his father. I think your colleague knows him?"

The girl glanced at the photograph and gave Mavis an old-fashioned look. "You mean Gary."

"Oh, you know him?"

"Couldn't help knowing him. I rent a room in Joyce's flat. Gary used to stay when he was passing through. . .it isn't a big flat."

"Did you ever meet Ben, his little boy?" The girl shook her head, looked at the proffered photos, and shook her head again.

"Didn't know he had a kid, to be honest. A wife, yes, back in England, that was the problem."

"He's divorced now," Mavis confided. "I hope your friend Joyce likes children because he's brought Ben—"

"Divorced? Gary? Oh, Jeez . . ." The girl sat abruptly and stared at Mavis. "When did that happen, for God's sake?"

"I'm not quite sure," Mavis admitted. "Before he came back to Australia."

"So how about that . . ." The news had obviously surprised her. Mr Pringle asked tentatively, "Do I take it, er, Joyce hadn't heard?"

"You take it," the girl said tonelessly. "In fact she'd given up hope of ever seeing him again. Did you tell her he was divorced when you saw her yesterday?"

"No," said Mr Pringle slowly, "I don't believe we did. We talked about the child rather than his parents."

"Maybe that was why Joyce cried most of last night, with you coming and talking about Gary and all." At their blank looks, she said, "You know where Joyce has gone today, don't you?"

"No?"

"She's left for Hobart. She's getting married on Saturday to a bloke she met through a dating agency, he's in pesticides." The girl fingered the photo. "He's dark, though. . .'fact, he's the nearest Joyce could find to Gary, know what I mean?"

"Oh, dear!" Mavis Bignell was sad. "That doesn't sound very promising."

By the end of half an hour, Mavis had polished off a "Wicked Lady" and come to terms with the situation. "Gary may have heard about Joyce's engagement, perhaps that's why he hasn't called, or maybe there was some other reason, but whatever it was, he must be earning his living. He's probably still driving lorries."

"Road trains," Charlie corrected. He'd rejoined them and was drinking the inevitable coke. "That's what they call the big long-distance trailer trucks out here."

"Ben must be at school," Mr Pringle pointed out. "A child doesn't travel round during term time."

"Ben missed such a lot of schooling at home," sighed Mavis, "because he was sickly." The waitress picked up another photo. "He looks a frail little thing. How old d'you say he was?"

Mr Pringle brooded. The pictures were fanned out in front of him. Were there special schools out here, for sickly children? Could Gary afford to send his child to one? The waitress confirmed Joyce's remark yesterday, that Gary was always "flat broke".

He looked up and found Charlie watching him. "I was thinking. . ."

"Yeah?"

"If one had a child requiring medical attention . . . the bills would be very heavy for a man like Gary."

"Could be," Charlie was non-committal. "He'd qualify for benefits—"

"Yes, but he might not know about those, not yet. And he'd be pretty desperate if he couldn't support the boy. Suppose he decided to foster Ben on a temporary basis, until he got a home together. How would Gary go about that?"

In the thirty-seater aircraft, Ray Vincent was beside a young mother with a pretty dark-haired daughter on her knee. The woman wore a sundress with panties underneath but little else and Vincent was uncomfortably aware of her body. He hadn't been in Australia long enough to become acclimatized; he thought of Adele instead, would she be safe as well as Amy?

The little girl had the same soapy smell Amy always had after her bath. She was about the same age but thinner and yellowy-tanned by the sun.

"Oh, Jesus!" The mother looked at him apologetically. "Sorry. I keep feeling sick. Kelly, stop bothering people!" Beneath the clinging cotton jersey of her sundress the nipples stood out. Ray Vincent made himself look her in the face. The child was wriggling to get down.

"Is your daughter shy of strangers or will she sit on my lap?"

"Are you sure you don't mind?" He smiled.

"I've got one of my own." It was against every rule, talking to strangers!

"Oh, well . . . if you're sure. Kelly, would you like to sit on the gentleman's knee?"

The little girl's hair was soft. She leaned docilely against his chest, a thumb in her mouth.

"I found out this morning I was pregnant," said her mother. "I was dreading flying after that."

"Congratulations."

"Yeah . . . Phil'll be pleased. We've got a farm. He wants a boy."

"What if it's another girl?" The mother smiled, her face softening.

"I shan't mind, I guess. Kelly, take your thumb out, darling."

For some time they didn't speak. The stewardess brought round small square trays of regulation sandwiches. Vincent and the woman took it in turns to eat.

"What's your little girl's name?" It was the child and it caught him off guard. Before he could stop himself, Ray Vincent heard himself say "Amy. . ."

After that, it was too late.

"There's one other thing you could try," said Charlie. Mavis sat beside him, dejection making her red curls droop.

"What's that, dear? I thought we'd phoned every single blessed adoption agency you knew in Sydney. I don't think I could go through explaining to anyone else today."

"No, not the kid, the father. You reckon he's still a truck driver, right?"

"As far as we know," said Mr Pringle.

"So why don't we ask them to call up on CB radio? All the truckers use it. Someone must know about him?"

"That's a good idea. Tomorrow," said Mavis, "when I've got my energy back, we'll find a nice-looking lorry driver and ask him to speak to his friends."

"Truckers. Out here that's what we call 'em."

"Well, yes . . ." said Mavis.

In Kev's room they were holding a council of war. "All we know for certain," said Kev, "is, number one: Evan Jones gave the seed packet two kilos of heroin and she still has it. Did you manage to get anything out of her?"

"Not a thing," Charlie admitted. "I tried. Asked about people she'd met on the flight, people who had contacts in Sydney, people who asked people to take things out for their friends—all she wanted to talk about was the kid.

"I know when he was born, when he first broke a leg,

everything. What she didn't want to talk about was how an airline steward gave her two bags of stuff and told her someone would be round to pick it up." Charlie took a pull on his beer.

"What about her partner?" asked Pelham-Walker.

"I thought Jones told you he wasn't involved?" Kev frowned.

"That's correct. But as they're obviously so close . . ." The motel walls didn't insulate the three of them from Mavis's laughter nor the occasional joyful chortle from G D H Pringle.

"At their age," said Charlie sourly, "it's disgusting."

"One day," Kev was stern, "*you*'ll be grateful you can still manage it. *If* you can. After wearing them tight jeans that strangle your balls for most of your life. Now, number two: Sydney can't tell us anything more about Ray Vincent 'cept what it has in his passport—and that he's been in Singapore a few times. Last visit when that guy was hanged in Penang."

"Oh yeah?" Charlie was alert. "Wasn't there a hint that guy might be reprieved?"

"My department had hopes initially," Pelham-Walker waved a deprecating hand. "There were insufficient grounds for an appeal, I fear."

"No," said Kev. "What Charlie was meanin' is why Vincent was around at the time the guy might have been let out. The organization don't have much time for blokes who get caught." He looked at Charlie who drew a thumb across his neck. "Right."

Pelham-Walker felt sick. "Surely not!"

"Look, get it out of your head Vincent's in real estate, Pelham. Not while he's carrying that gun, he isn't. Brisbane are still tryin' to find him, by the way. And we got no result on Byers Street except it's always been let to missionaries."

"I see."

"So what's the news your end?"

"Evan Jones was brutally murdered—in stages apparently."

"You mean he was tortured?" Anthony Pelham-Walker shied away from such an unpleasant word. "The poor bastard," Kev grumbled. "Didn't the bloody fools your end realize he was our only witness? Why the hell couldn't you protect the poor bugger?" Pelham-Walker patted his mouth with a handkerchief.

"I have done what I can to help," he said, attempting dignity. "I have instructed Crispin Sinclair to find out what he can about Ray Vincent. It isn't his field, of course, but he will do his best."

"Any idea who killed Jones yet? Any names?" asked Charlie.

"That sort of evidence takes weeks or months to sift through." This made Kev angry.

"They must act quicker 'n that! We don't want the same thing to happen to the Bignell lady."

"I don't see how there can possibly be a connection. Two men were involved in Evan Jones's case. Traces of saliva and sweat found at the cottage—"

"Two? Pelham, d'you think for once in a bloody while you could tell me the whole of the information, 'stead of keeping little titbits back!" The roar unnerved him. "We been lookin' for one bloke—now you tell me there's two of 'em!"

"I'm so sorry, I never thought . . ." Anthony Pelham-Walker flapped his hands helplessly. He was dishevelled after two days on the road. Any lingering aura of Whitehall authority had completely disappeared. The eyes were dull in his thin face and the tightly pursed mouth twitched constantly. "I fear I'm not exactly suited . . . My milieu, my *métier* even, is to be situate in an office, away from unnecessary pressures. I'm much more accustomed to making rational decisions after consideration of all known facts—"

"Yeah?" sneered Kev. "Like not to offer protection to Jones? Well there's no bloody office and it was your decision to involve yourself, not mine, Pelham. You are in this now, whether you like it or not, and we're all the protection that Bignell lady's got, apart from Charlie, so start doin' some of that rational thinkin' you're good at, and do it quick!"

Suddenly the bronze equine buttocks, Greenwich, even a drunken Fiona, became very desirable objects. Anthony Pelham-Walker was saved from further wrath by the telephone.

"Yes? Oh, great!" Kev's left fist clenched with frustration. "Well, keep tryin'. Whatever you do, don't give up because we gotta find him . . . Yeah, yeah . . . It's a hard life!" He banged the receiver down. "Bloody Queenslanders!"

"What's up?"

"They think they gotta a lead on Vincent at a hotel in Brisbane but he checked out four hours ago."

"Did he leave a forwarding address?" asked Pelham-Walker, interested.

Dear God, don't let me kill him! Kev's knuckles cracked under the tension.

In their comfortable room Mavis couldn't sleep. The other bedside light was still on. "What are you doing?"

"Looking at the pictures of Ben. In over half of them he has some injury or other."

"I told you, he was always having accidents. Mrs Hardie visited that hospital ward—"

"Was there ever an investigation? As to why?" Mavis rolled over and looked at him.

"You mean—whether it always was accidental?" Her eyes grew round. "Mrs Hardie doted on him, he was her only grandchild."

"No, I meant his parents, Linda and Gary." She sat up indignantly.

"That's a bit strong, isn't it? What you're suggesting?"

"Child abuse isn't unknown. Everyone claims it was an unhappy marriage."

"Yes, but not because of Ben. Gary worshipped the boy."

"And—Linda?" This made Mavis uneasy.

"Linda liked a good time, not staying at home. Mrs Hardie was always baby-sitting, or Gary. He didn't go drinking much." She considered the implication but shook her head. "I think you're wrong. I can't see Linda deliberately injuring her baby."

"Just a thought," Mr Pringle said mildly, "Because Ben seems to have been so remarkably unfortunate."

"I've been awake, too, thinking about that powder. You still think someone might come for it, don't you? I was wondering about Charlie actually."

"Good heavens!"

Mavis sighed. She didn't like to think ill of anyone with such muscular brown legs. The way men wore shorts all the time out here was lovely! Then she remembered how she'd been beguiled by Evan's blue eyes. What a blasted nuisance it was, growing old. It made you lose your marbles, gave you a weight problem and

119

stopped you enjoying yourself. When she spoke again, she sounded irritable.

"The truth is I don't know if I'm right. But I got to turning over in my mind what you said at Sydney. After we'd had that bit of a spat. 'Be suspicious from now on . . .'—d'you remember?"

"Yes, I do."

"Well Charlie only joined the trip that morning and you could see Pete hadn't met him before, the way they shook hands. Then today, while you were zizzing away in the back, he asked me ever such a lot of funny questions. More hints, really. About people I might have met on the trip."

"Oh dear." Mr Pringle had almost forgotten about it because of Ben. Now, fear returned in abundance. He'd be lucky if he managed a wink of sleep after this. "I wonder if we should contact the police after all?"

"Not on your nelly," Mrs Bignell said stoutly. "We're giving Evan a chance to go straight first. And anyway, just suppose he—Charlie—is the police?"

"Oh, crikey!"

"Not that I think it's very likely," she added comfortably. "I think he's more likely to be one of *them*, come for the powder like you said. Whatever he is, I think we should be very careful and keep our distance, don't you?"

"Absolutely."

Bother! thought Mavis. She'd been honest but it hadn't done her any good. Wasn't that always the way? All the scrumptious things in life were bad for you, like cream cakes. Then she remembered with a sense of shame that she was already beloved, and cherished, and had no further need of handsome young men. "Tell you what," she offered in expiation, "how about a cup of tea? There's milk and digestives in the fridge. You stay where you are, I'll make it."

When she leaned over to put the cup on the bedside table, her breasts were close enough for him to kiss. As he thanked her, Mr Pringle murmured gently, "You will take great care, won't you, Mavis?"

Chapter Fifteen

Crispin Sinclair made the one-way race circuit of Farnham a second time, looking for an empty space. In the end he surrendered and drove into a car-park. There was a lunch-time jazz session erupting from the foyer of the Redgrave Theatre. Elderly ladies pushing shoppers from Sainsbury's across to the bus-stop walked past the noise with disapproving sniffs.

"They require," Batman had said, "information concerning a Mr Ray Vincent, a British subject working as an estate agent. They need a photograph and any other details you can discover. Vincent is in Australia at present . . ." He paused but decided against giving his subordinate further information. "This time, Sinclair," he added sharply, "I shall expect results."

"Yes, sir. Is there any chance you'll be returning shortly? There has been a certain amount of—speculation—in the department—" But Batman had hung up. Sod him, thought Crispin, leaving me to face the music.

The flat oppressed him. Ever since lover-boy's departure the sound of the phone gave him the jitters and he refused to answer the door unless the caller's voice was one he knew. He'd be safer looking for Vincent; outside he'd be anonymous.

There was no R Vincent listed as an estate agent. A bored telephonist commented, "He's probably trading under another name. D'you know if he lives in the Greater London area?"

"Quite likely, I'd say."

"Shall I transfer you to Directory Enquiries? His home number might be easier to trace?" But this time there were hundreds of R Vincents. Crispin phoned his ex-lover at the FO.

"I thought you'd have been killed by now."

"You left some of your discs behind. I'll smash them if you don't get me some information."

"Bitch!"

"I want an address and phone number from the passport office or Australia House. This chap renewed a visa recently."

In the end, his lover could only come up with the name of a town. Crispin scratched his initials on each of the discs before putting them in the post.

He pushed open the door of the *Farnham Advertiser*. "I wonder if you happen to have photographs of one of our local celebrities?" He smiled charmingly at the middle-aged lady behind the counter. "It's his wedding anniversary next month. Some of us are planning a *This is Your Life* kind of thing. I've been detailed to find pictures for the album."

"We might have." She'd opened an old-fashioned card index.

"It's Mr Ray Vincent. He's an estate agent. You don't happen to know him yourself, by any chance?"

At the Orano Windmill Motel in Gilgandra, the FONEs settled down to enjoy their final night in comfortable beds before going camping. The tour was to proceed after all. Protheroe knew that to justify the subsidized cost, he had to return with proof of their efforts. On the other hand, there was no point in being unnecessarily heroic.

"From now on, there will be no public meetings which the press can gatecrash. We shall hold informal gatherings in the bush," he announced.

"Outback," murmured one who was better informed.

"Ah, yes. Outback. When we get to the campsites or isolated settlements we can offer to answer any questions the locals may have . . . Reassure them, that kind of thing. These meetings will be logged of course but will be impromptu to avoid any further adverse reporting by the, er, media." Fellow physicists nodded. To a man, they understood.

"Adam Lithgoe" stood under a shower for several minutes. Wearing only a towel, he padded quietly along to the hotel laundry room and took his clothes out of the machine. A housewife would've thrown up her hands in horror; new, white T-shirts now had blotchy stains from the seersucker jacket.

Ray Vincent appeared satisfied. He didn't hang them to dry outside, though, but on a line in his room. Dressing in business clothes once more and with opaque sunglasses, he set off to make a few necessary purchases. He had to visit a bank, which made him edgy because it meant leaving a record of the transaction, but there was no way round it, he needed a hefty amount of cash.

In a sports shop, the assistant was sympathetic over the loss of his binoculars. "Can't put anything down nowadays . . . folks just aren't honest any more. These are nice and neat. Useful as night-glasses."

"Fine."

Ray Vincent worked his way along the street, mentally checking off his list. When the last item was purchased he ate a hefty steak at a snack-bar before returning for another long shower; he hated not to be clean. The stubble on his chin was itchy now because he hadn't shaved since yesterday. He resisted the urge to scratch as he checked out.

"That was a short visit, Mr Lithgoe." The receptionist smiled in a friendly fashion. Ray Vincent grimaced.

"Summons from head office. You know how it is . . ."

Once outside, he moved smartly to where his final purchase, a rusty Volkswagen, was parked. Checking a compass against the map for a few miles, to be certain it was accurate, he drove west out of Broken Hill.

Mrs Hardie was using metal crutches supplied by the hospital and catching hold of each familiar piece of furniture. It was late and only the day following the welfare lady's visit but she was in a fever to complete her arrangements. Ollie Gorman filled her kitchen as usual. She sat, for safety's sake, leaning the crutches against the table.

"You're doing marvellous," he assured her loudly, "and you're looking so well. Now—" A notebook was in one hand, a stubby pencil in the other "—as I see it, what you need is a van with a Luton top—that's the boxy bit above the driver—where we put the beds."

"Bed," Mrs Hardie corrected him. "I'm only taking the one. I'm leaving the rest for Linda."

"All the same, you'll need a Luton if you're going to take that sideboard."

"Yes." She wouldn't part with it; not much had survived her marriage but her mother had saved every penny to give her that.

"Lovely piece of furniture . . ." Ollie spoke automatically as he totted up figures. "Now, we got a choice. If it's a weekday, it'll have to be two small vans—I'll have to pay one of the drivers the going rate, can't lay my hands on two vans you see." He sucked in air at the size of the total. "Fifty-eight, say sixty-five with beer money. If it was a Sunday, now, my brother-in-law'd do it. He can borrow his boss's van. It's big, only need the one. That'd work out much cheaper."

"I don't want anything illegal."

"He'd replace the petrol." Ollie was wide-eyed. "Engines ought to be used every day otherwise the batteries go flat. Thirty quid. Say, thirty-five, to cover incidentals."

"All right."

"These bits and pieces of yours . . . little ornaments, photos and such. We couldn't be responsible for the packing. Can Linda give you a hand?"

"Linda mustn't know," Mrs Hardie said quickly. "I told you before."

"So you did," Ollie pacified her. "I'd forgotten."

"It's important."

"OK, I'll remember. But can you manage?"

"Yes . . . I'll ask my home help. She doesn't mind earning a bit extra." Ollie Gorman's glance had strayed across to the mantle-piece.

"I see Mavie's keeping you well supplied with postcards. Has she come across Ben yet?"

"No . . ."

"Never mind, she'll keep trying. We got a pc from her at The Bricklayers. Said she'd been picked up by ever such a nice young man on the aircraft. Old Pringle'd better watch out." Ollie leered. "That bar isn't the same without Mavie, you know. Even the beer tastes flat. Your Linda's been in plenty . . . enjoying herself."

"Listen, Ollie, you will be careful what you say? Not even a hint?"

"Cross my heart and hope to die. When d'you want the job done?"

"I should know by the end of the week."

"So what's the seed packet decided to do today?" Charlie stood in the open doorway of Kev's room from where he could watch the restaurant unobserved.

"Pringle's been doing the sums. I heard him say they could afford one more day in the hire-car then they got to catch up with the coaches. They were discussing looking for this Gary character rather than the kid, they reckon he might be easier to locate."

"Sounds reasonable," said Kev. "The kid's most likely back in Sydney if his father's on the road."

"*If* he's still got a job. Anythin' from Brisbane yet?"

"Nuthin'." Kev was disgusted. He switched off his electric shaver and came to stand behind Charlie. "So . . . one more day then they rejoin the tour?"

"Looks like it."

"When she'll be where *they* expect to find her . . . and a long way from home, where I think they'll come out into the open and go for it."

"You don't think . . . I mean, she's no idea what could be comin' to her, Kev."

"She's the only bait we've got. We can't let her in on it, she couldn't act the decoy convincingly. She'd start havin' the vapours every time she saw a strange man. Besides, you'll be up there with her."

"Yeah."

"With me and Pelham right behind you."

Jean Protheroe marvelled at the flat arid landscape. Fifty-seven miles according to Pete, with a rise of only seventeen feet. Worse than Lincolnshire. Blazing heat made the window hot to the touch and showed up the grey under her auburn rinse. "How long could a man survive out there, Kenneth?"

"Depends how much water he had in his billy-can," he said playfully. "Notice the mirage?"

"One can scarcely miss it, it's gone on for miles. Are we stopping for coffee today?"

"Somewhere called Cobar. It's a copper town."

"As long as it has air conditioning, that's all I ask."

He waited in the Volkswagen, screened from view behind scrubby spinifex. Ray Vincent wore shorts and one of the mottled T-shirts. Dust from his all-night drive covered his hair and clothes as well as the car. Sweat caked it deep into the wrinkles on his face, etching a pattern of weariness.

He saw the moving billowing dust, the glint of red and white—it must be them, they'd finally got here! As both coaches swept past, he scanned the passengers, gripping the binoculars fiercely.

The only red-head was in the second coach. He picked up the sugar and slipped along unobtrusively, keeping in the deep black shadow of verandahs until he was close to where they were parked.

It was too hot for coffee. Across the street was the Western Hotel with the longest verandah in New South Wales, according to Pete. They began to drift across. As soon as the first disappeared inside, momentum increased. "It's open!"

"Mine's a lager, two if we've got time."

"Two? I could drink the place dry!"

"Goin' for a slash and a cold coke, mate," said Pete.

"Right. Sheri and me'll clear this lot then we'll join you." Lenny began stacking unwanted urns and crockery back into the belly of his vehicle. Ray Vincent moved swiftly and unscrewed the filler cap on the adjacent coach.

In the pub, Pete was discussing the route ahead with Protheroe. "We can stay in Wilcannia if you like. See what you think when we get there. Or we can push on to Broken Hill."

"Anything wrong with Wilcannia?"

"We-ll . . ." Pete was reluctant to do his country down. "It used to be an important sort of a town . . . all that's changed. It's got a kind of hopeless feel to it nowadays."

"We can reach it in time for a late lunch?"

"Sure. Sheri's got everything organized. We can keep goin' as long as you like."

"Let's see it, then decide." Protheroe looked at his watch. "Time ladies and gentlemen, if you please."

They went in convoy, Lenny in the lead. From time to time he and Pete chatted over their radio. The horizon stretched endlessly ahead, Cobar had disappeared. Outside, the sun reached its zenith.

"She's coughing a lot, mate . . . snatching, too."

"Muck in the carburettor?"

"Nah . . ." The engine surged then missed and Pete pressed his foot down. "Somethin's odd though."

"Want to stop?"

"You keep goin'. You and Sheri see to the dinner. I'll nurse the old girl along."

The coach bucked under the pressure of his foot then juddered to a halt. "Just goin' to take a look, folks. Maybe a 'roo's got jammed in the works."

There was nothing on the horizon except the disappearing dust that was Lenny's coach, and the flies.

"Can't he leave the fan on to keep it cool! That might help." Up and down the coach, frantic arms holding *New Scientists* flailed ineffectually.

"It's so hot! Absolutely stifling!"

Lying in the road beneath the crankshaft, Pete saw feet wander past. "Hey! Come back." He slithered out wiping the oil from his face. "It's dangerous to wander off. If you must come outside, stay in the shade."

Ten minutes driving time behind, Ray Vincent turned off the highway and drove along a dried-up river bed. Silver-white ghost gums shielded him from view. When he judged he'd travelled far enough, he stopped, took up the binoculars and crawled to the level of the road.

The FONEs were huddled in a narrow strip of shade beside the coach. The emergency barrel of water was out and the driver was shouting at them to sip, not gulp each precious cupful. Ray Vincent slithered back down behind the protecting scrub and doubled back to his car.

He took out his own two-gallon can, soaked a towel and

wrapped it round his head. He wet his lips but didn't swallow and settled down to wait.

In Wilcannia, lunch was nearly over. They lolled under trees in the drab municipal park. One or two sat on the swings. Lenny checked his watch again; over an hour. Time to find out what was happening.

"OK, folks, if you've finished, there's the Darling river in that direction. Plenty of wild life if you like that kind of thing but keep out of the sun. The bar's open in the hotel over there. Any problems, see Sheri. Back soon as I can."

Pete was struggling to keep discipline. "Please do as I ask. None of you are used to this kind of heat. Please, folks . . . Come back inside and I'll run the fan for five minutes. Keep as still as you can to conserve energy."

"Can I have some more water?" He looked at his watch.

"None yet, sorry."

"Why can't you call the AA or something?" asked Protheroe angrily. The chorus was taken up.

"Surely you can use that radio to speak to a garage!" Pete tried not to grin because his lips felt ready to split.

"Maybe you haven't noticed . . . we don't have that many garages. Lenny'll be here soon."

When the other coach eventually pulled up, some of the FONEs ran across half hysterically, desperate to be cool. Lenny crouched down beside his partner.

"What's the trouble?"

"Dirty fuel, I reckon. Which is bloody odd considerin' she's been goin' all right. She went sweet as a nut up to Cobar."

"So it's a breakdown job?"

"I'd say so. You'll need to get those Poms out of the sun pretty soon. Can't tow this old girl as well." Lenny knew he was right but it didn't make it any easier.

"Protheroe'll wet his knickers. I'll see what's available to come out from Wilcannia. You stayin' here?"

"Yeah," Pete growled. "Might as well start emptyin' her. I'll leave the radio switched on."

128

"Right. Got enough water?"

"Yeah."

Ray Vincent felt dizzy. He tried to focus on what was happening through the heat haze. Passengers were climbing aboard the other coach which reversed and set off back towards Wilcannia. Great!

He swallowed the cupful of water he had beside him in the scrub, he could afford the luxury this time, and not bothering at concealment ran back to his car.

His watch felt loose on his sweaty wrist. He paused to tighten it and didn't notice Pete dip underneath the coach once more.

The Volkswagen roared to a halt beside the luggage compartment. Vincent was out, tugging at the handle. It took him by surprise because it wasn't locked. He didn't stop to think but flung the flap upright against the side of the coach and began heaving suitcases on to the road.

"Good of you to stop, mate—" Pete froze as Vincent swung round. "Bloody hell—!" The wrench caught him on the side of the neck and his head crashed against the unyielding metal coachwork. Pete's legs folded and his body tipped forward into the dust.

"Christ!" Ray Vincent wanted to keep on hitting, to annihilate the knowledge in Pete that he'd seen him. He kicked the body on to its back; eyes stared upward, seeing nothing. He gave the head another hard blow and began emptying the suitcases.

Sweat blinded him; it wasn't here! Wreckage was strewn over the road. Clothes were heaped among the slashed luggage. She'd got the stuff with her, it was the only possible explanation. Worse, she obviously knew what it was, otherwise she'd have it in her suitcase. Jones had sworn he hadn't told her—a man facing death doesn't lie. But the steward hadn't picked a stupid old tart, he'd found one that had her wits about her.

Ray Vincent bundled the wreckage into the hold in a fury. Inside the coach he slit open every remaining package but it wasn't there either. He didn't want to kill her; he'd gone to all this trouble to avoid it, but now. . .she'd signed her own death warrant.

A crackle on the radio brought him to his senses. He rushed out, leaping clumsily into the road. The Volkswagen still throbbed and, as a last vicious gesture, Ray Vincent kicked the driver's body so that it lay in the full glare of the sun.

He drove recklessly until the outskirts of Wilcannia. There was no other choice of route, he had to go through it. Instinct made him slow down. He'd have to go back to Broken Hill and risk being recognized. Ray Vincent was forced to consider his alternative plan. He had to get ahead of the tour which meant driving day and night as far as Port Augusta. That was the only way to gain enough time.

Sweat soaked the plastic seat. He'd planned to do it without killing because a bullet could hamper his escape. The organization were angry because the route had dried up but even they agreed, once Jones was dead, there was no point in killing the woman. Not after Vincent had been able to assure them Jones knew nothing more. Vincent's task was to retrieve the two kilos and get out leaving no traces.

Then Zee had told him about the Home Office connection. Jones hadn't said a word about that. What else had he managed to withhold despite the agony? If Parker hadn't gone berserk, they could've got it out of him.

Ray Vincent cursed savagely. Another corpse and his luck could run out. Amy! Had he killed that dumb idiot of a driver? His skull was cracked, enough to stop him talking. Long enough for Vincent to find the woman. She had to die.

The police officer eased his gut out of the driving seat and stood, elbows resting on the roof. The farm dog was announcing his arrival loudly enough.

A young woman pushed open the mesh door and called, "Yes? I'm bathing my little girl." He walked across slowly. This property was remote and he didn't want to make her nervous.

"Mrs Chrissie Cartwell?"

"That's right."

"My ID, Mrs Cartwell." He waited. She examined it carefully. Inside, he could hear the little girl splashing about.

"I'll wait out here if you prefer, Mrs Cartwell."

"No, it's OK. I'm in the kitchen." She went ahead of him,

sweeping her daughter up in the towel and lifting her out of the tin bath. "What's the problem? My car insurance?"

"I believe you were on a flight from Brisbane to Broken Hill coupla days ago? We're checking all the passengers on that flight."

"My word! That was a full load."

"It was, Mrs Cartwell. Luckily 'bout twelve of 'em came from the same firm. Makes life easier. Now according to this—" He showed her the photostat of the seating plan "—you were in a window seat, 8A, with your little girl on your knee, right?" The woman nodded.

"Boy, I felt crook that day."

"What about the passenger in 8B, name of Judd?"

"He helped me with Kelly."

"Remember anythin' about him? What'd he look like, for instance?"

"God, what is this? Was he a rapist, or what?"

"Not as far as we know." The policeman tried to keep it avuncular. "Just been told to find out all we can. What colour hair, can you remember?"

"Fair, I think . . ." Chrissie Cartwell pushed her own out of her eyes and reached for Kelly's nightdress. "Yes, he was fairer than you."

"Tall?"

"Not very. Middling like Phil, my husband. Broader though. He looked—like he enjoyed his food a lot."

"A gut you mean?" She laughed.

"Well . . ."

"I get it, not as big as mine. Did he look like an outdoor sort of fella?" Chrissie frowned.

"He might've been once, with that build. I think he was some kind of salesman. He'd got one of those zip-up briefcases. To do with plastics, I think."

"That's real observant of you, Mrs Cartwell." He was about to ask another question when there was a shout.

"He was smelly!" Kelly was peeping over her mother's shoulder. "Smelly man!" she yelled again. Chrissie Cartwell laughed.

"Certainly was! I told you I was feeling crook? Some of those

131

men's toiletries, they really set me off. Kelly's the same. Takes after me, except she's not pregnant." The officer nodded sympathetically.

"Any idea what it was? What brand?"

"No . . . it was woody, sort of musky. Powerful. Oh, and another thing—he'd got a daughter, too. Told Kelly her name was Amy. That any use?"

"Sure." He waited patiently as Chrissie Cartwell searched her memory for a final item that eluded her.

"Yes, that was it . . . he seemed like a proud father. He was really fond of that little girl."

"It's been a lovely day. I'm only sorry we haven't come across Gary but you never know—" Mavis was as optimistic as ever "—with all those lorry drivers calling each other on their CBs, we still might. I gave them our whereabouts."

Yeah, thought Charlie gloomily, just about the whole of Australia knows where you're goin', lady, so let's keep our fingers crossed.

"One of them told me he'd come across several Pommies driving those road trains."

"Poms," Charlie corrected, "or Pommie bastards, that's how we say it." Mavis took it in her stride.

"It's an interesting language, isn't it, full of subtle nuances? And it's very kind of *you* to do all the driving, dear." In the cool of the morning, Mrs Bignell had changed her mind about Charlie. He couldn't possibly be a drug trafficker and she couldn't see him as a policeman. He was simply a driver who knew the road far better than they did. "Mr Pringle's catching up on his beauty sleep!" she murmured.

He'd done nothing but sleep, the randy old sod! Charlie glanced in the mirror. Mr Pringle's head was tilted back and his mouth open. When he wheezed occasionally, his moustache twitched. He'd been like that for the best part of three hundred and fifty miles.

It was dusk and far behind he could see Kev's headlights. At the last roadhouse, they'd managed a snatched urgent conversation. "Whoever it is, he's out in the open—Pete's been attacked, I've been talking to the police at Wilcannia."

132

"Christ!"

"Can't stop—she's looking this way. Lenny's takin' the rest of 'em to the campsite at Broken Hill, that's where we'll go next." Charlie did a quick calculation.

"That's a bloody long way!" But Kev had disappeared.

When she was told, Mavis didn't object. Another long drive would be lovely. There would be a full moon later on, very romantic. She'd done her best to find Gary, her conscience was clear; from now on she could simply sit back and enjoy her holiday.

The coach had been towed away. They drove unwittingly over the stretch of road where the flying doctor's aircraft landed earlier. When they paused for a meal in Wilcannia, they learned all about it in the pub.

It was a beer-swilling place where Aborigines sat drinking silently, watching others who simply passed through. Charlie kept his eyes on Mavis Bignell's face as the bartender gave them the details then, making his excuses, he went to stand in the urinal next to Kev.

"She was genuinely upset. No sign she's worked out what the bloke was really lookin' for."

"Good," said Kev softly. "He's bound to try again. Tomorrow they're travelling to Coober Pedy; day after that, Ayers Rock. That'll be his last chance. After that, the Poms are due to go home."

"You still reckon it's this Vincent bloke?" Kev shrugged.

"Dunno. The office are sending all they've got to Woomera. That's tomorrow's coffee stop. We might find somethin' interesting waitin' for us. Meanwhile, Charlie my son, you just keep your eyes peeled as far as Broken Hill."

"Yeah . . ." Charlie indicated Pelham-Walker hidden in a cubicle. "The mother country come up with anythin'?"

"Give 'em a chance. They're probably down to usin' bikes by this time, to save the pennies."

An embarrassed police force had done their best. The FONEs had been soothed, Protheroe was deferred to and a forty-seater coach put at Lenny's disposal. The red and white Wallaby vehicles would be left in Wilcannia and Charlie's was already being repaired.

What mattered was that the rest of their holiday should be as smooth as possible because nothing like this had happened before and they were anxious to avoid bad publicity.

After the first burst of anger, the British told each other vandalism was the same all over the world. Their belongings were stowed temporarily in paper sacks. Once they were in Broken Hill, they'd been told to purchase new luggage and the state would foot the bill.

"Generous, really," said Protheroe, "all things considered. I doubt whether we'd have done the same for any Australians visiting Bournemouth."

"No one would attack a coach in Bournemouth!"

"I don't know . . . These days."

"I think we should organize a whip-round," Jean Protheroe insisted. "From what Lenny told me, Pete's in a bad way."

Outside the operating theatre in Alice Springs, Pete implored with his eyes but couldn't speak. "A Volks'," he begged silently. "He was driving a Volks'." The anaesthetist picked up a needle.

"Just a prick, you'll hardly feel a thing." Ten seconds later, Pete was unconscious.

They drove into Broken Hill at sunset. Ochre soil and scrub had given way to bungalows surrounded by lawns and trees. As usual the contrast was startling. Further into town there were shacks close to the mines and, on the far side, the campsite itself.

There was excitement, voices had a confident ring. Hearing them, Lenny managed a smile. "Maybe you'd like Sheri and me to show you how to pitch the first tent?"

In the scramble to unload, sleeping-bags, tents and airbeds were tossed out feverishly. Beyond the mêlée, Sheri had started up the barbecue and the fragrance of grilling steaks added to the urgency.

"We pitch them in a line," Lenny instructed. "Each shares two pegs with the next tent and so on. No gaps, right? You connect the centre pole, push it up the middle to support the roof—and there you are."

It was so simple: a heap of canvas transformed into a modest sentry-box of a dwelling in a twinkle. Lenny hammered home four pegs and it was done. Scientists and physicists looked at one another in amusement: how could their combined Oxbridge talents fail to cope with that?

Protheroe began the rout by shouting at Jean. Up and down the site, others followed suit, bawling, yelling, seizing mallets, grabbing inflatable mattresses and disputing possession of sleeping-bags. Bedlam reigned as a half-crazed army of generals issued commands to mutinous spouses.

When it was over, the line of tents snaked uncertainly, sagging roofs a drunken silhouette against the night sky. Arriving a few hours later when all was quiet, Mr Pringle surveyed it and shook his head. He began erecting their tent as quietly as possible. Mrs. Bignell sat on a stool in the moonlight to watch.

"I do think you're clever," she whispered. "Ours is the only one that's upright. But why is the opening on the opposite side to everyone else?"

"I fancy none of them have noticed they're facing east. Sunrise is about five a.m." He held open the flap and she crawled inside.

"I'm so glad you're not a nuclear physicist, dear."

Charlie clambered into the empty hold of the coach where he was to sleep. Lenny lay there waiting, smoking a cigarette. "We've got somethin' to discuss." Charlie groaned.

"Can't it wait?"

"No it bloody well can't!" Lenny hissed. "Someone nobbles a coach, nearly kills my best mate, all because somethin's happenin' that I don't know about. And don't give me any crap about it's these Poms and their silly ideas upsettin' a nutcase, because it bloody well doesn't add up! So what's going on?" Charlie told him.

At the finish, Lenny stubbed out his cigarette. "You bastards owe me one coach and driver and one hell of an apology—"

"I'll drive," Charlie said quickly. "I'll do Pete's share."

"Too right you bloody will," Lenny agreed, "and you'll pay compensation if the poor bugger dies." He looked at Charlie speculatively. "You forgot to tell me the important bit, didn't you?" Charlie didn't reply. Lenny leaned across.

135

"What you forgot to say was—that wasn't the end of it. This maniac's gonna try again. Isn't he?"

In their tent, Mr Pringle waited until he heard Mavis's regular breathing before easing himself out of his sleeping-bag. Thank heavens he'd managed to doze earlier. In Wilcannia, he'd been too shocked by the news to speak. Seeing that Mavis hadn't grasped its significance, he'd decided not to upset her. Tomorrow, in private, he would persuade her they must go to the police. Tonight he would defend her against all comers.

G D H Pringle wasn't a brave man. He'd no intention of engaging an attacker, but he could raise the alarm if necessary and to do that meant staying awake. He sighed. It was the only way. At least he could look at the stars.

Pulling on a sweater and with his scout knife, Mr Pringle unzipped the flap and went outside. Alas for heroism! Up and down the row, the FONEs were wide awake in the unfamiliar surroundings, reliving earlier acrimony or acting out marital fantasy.

Sitting there, it became impossible to concentrate on the universe. Who on earth was addressing his soulmate loudly as "Mrs Piggybum"? Surely not that elderly academic who was always complaining about the food?

As he shook his head over other embarrassments, wondering how on earth they would face each other in the morning, there was an explosive shout. Mr Pringle seized his knife but it was only Protheroe, savaged by mosquitoes. He erupted out of his tent at the other end of the line, knocking down the pole. Mr Pringle watched sadly as sagging rigging gave way and domino effect took over. Irate tousled heads began to emerge. At least Mrs Bignell was safe, he reflected.

Chapter Sixteen

The inquest into the unlawful killing of Evan Jones was soon over without revealing any of the details the press were so eager to hear. One witness, Crispin Sinclair, exhibited a skill in avoiding pitfalls which brought forth praise.

"Most satisfactory . . ." The atmosphere inside the limousine taking him and the acting HOD back to London was cordial.

"Thank you, sir."

"Despite Pelham-Walker's aberration, I think we can claim the department has salvaged its most precious possession ... its reputation." Crispin remained modestly silent.

There was a suggestion of a cough from the official, a clearing of the throat that heralded a delicate matter for discussion. "Re the subject of Pelham-Walker—and this must go no further, Sinclair."

"Yes, sir?"

"A decision has been taken which, given the circumstances, was inevitable I fear . . ."

Evan's mother and sister were driven home by sympathetic police. The WPC lingered in the chilly hall. "You will stay with your mam. You won't leave her on her own?" Evan's sister nodded.

"She hasn't been left since it happened." The policewoman looked relieved.

"At least they've released the body for burial. Maybe she'll find some comfort, being able to grieve properly."

"The doctor gave her some pills." The daughter was doubtful. "She's been like a zombie since . . . I don't think she knows what's going on."

"Poor thing," the WPC murmured. "I'll keep in touch, love. As soon as there's a hint they've got the men who did it, I'll come round. OK?"

The girl returned to where her mother sat in the kitchen. "Would you like a nice cup of tea, Mam?" Her mother roused herself.

"That was him, wasn't it? That found Evan? The last person to see him alive?"

"That's right." The girl waited. Eventually her mam said, "I just wanted to be sure."

It was an early start at Broken Hill. Mr Pringle's social standing had risen a couple of points; theirs was the only tent which hadn't collapsed during the night. If Mrs Bignell hadn't been so obdurate concerning the police, he might have relished the situation even more.

"Look, dear, we can't be sure it was one of the drug people who wrecked the coach. Why did he hit Pete on the head if he was? Jean Protheroe said the police thought it was straightforward vandalism, they were very apologetic about it."

"Mavis, we must tell someone!"

"All right," she capitulated. "I'll finish that letter to Evan. When we get to Coober Pedy we'll find a post-office and after that—if anything else happens—we'll tell someone. That do?"

It was a compromise but it didn't make his cornflakes taste any better.

His nerve was shaken again when they paused for coffee at Yunta, a hald with two roadhouses and six small dwellings. Mr Pringle was determined not to let Mrs Bignell out of his sight but having sampled ice-cream in one café, she decided it might taste even better on the other side of the road. Mr Pringle lingered behind, anxious for a private word with Lenny.

"This youngster my friend is so anxious to trace . . ."

"Yes?" Since Charlie's revelation about Mavis Lenny's manner towards both of them was guarded. Fortunately Mr Pringle appeared unaware.

"The boy enjoyed poor health and had missed a great deal of schooling. Would the authorities out here insist he attend a remedial school in the circumstances? And would there be a way of finding out once we return to Sydney?" Lenny's eyebrows rose.

"Search me," he admitted honestly. "You could be right, but I'm blessed if I know who to ask—hallo? Looks like your friend's found herself a pal over there—"

What happened next took him completely by surprise. Mr Pringle shot across the road at twice the speed he would expect from a man his age, and stood panting between Mrs Bignell and a bewildered truck driver.

It was less of a shock to see Charlie already there, one hand inside his jacket, but Lenny still swore. That Bignell lady was dynamite; the sooner this whole trip was over, the better. Lenny had screwed a promise of compensation for Pete's injuries out of Charlie in return for co-operation, but thank God there were only three more days to go.

"Yes?" gasped Mr Pringle. The truck driver was massive and towered over him.

"I was only askin' if she was the party looking for the Pom. She fitted the description and this is the Wallaby Tours outfit, ain't it?"

"It's all right, dear. This isn't about you know what . . ." Mavis was stopped by his expression as Mr Pringle whipped round. "I mean, it's about Gary," she finished lamely. She smiled up at the driver. "Have you found him on your CB?"

"Not exactly. Not many Poms drivin' road trains, nowadays. There's one we all know 'bout, though. Got his own business in Perth. He uses other Poms as truckers when he can."

"How far's Perth from here?" asked Mavis. He was astonished.

"'Bout two thousand five hundred kilometres due west."

"Oh, dear." Even Mavis realized it was impossible.

"That can't be Gary," Mr Pringle insisted. "He hadn't got a job when he came back, remember." He turned to the trucker. "I'm sorry if I appeared abrupt. One of our coaches was involved in an incident yesterday." The huge Australian was already shaking his head.

"Shockin'," he told them. "Never heard anythin' like it before . . . Everyone's been talkin' 'bout it. Been on the national news and everythin'."

"The other Pommies?" asked Mavis. "Are any of them nearer than Perth?"

"Yeah, that's what I came to tell you 'bout. One of 'em was headed for Coober Pedy last night. You might find it's him when you get there." Mavis glowed.

"How splendid! Would you like an ice-cream? I was just going to have another one." Charlie watched them disappear. Now why did old Pringle react like that if he didn't know about the stuff? It didn't add up.

He was still brooding about it when he joined Kev during the tea-stop at Woomera. They were at the disused launch site, dotted with concrete plinths each topped with an empty rocket. The site symbolized more than a forgotten era to the FONEs. Physicists wandered among the defunct exhibits crying aloud in happy recognition. "Those things were goin' to protect Australia once upon a time," said Kev. "Now look at 'em. Just scrap metal."

"Yeah." Charlie hadn't reached the age of nostalgia. "Listen, Kev—"

"Later, Charlie, when we're at Coober Pedy. We've not got much time before the coach leaves and there's this mass of stuff come from Macquarie Street. Pelham's bloke finally got permission to use a carrier pigeon, too. Look at these." Kev pulled photographs out of a pile.

"So that's what Vincent looks like nowadays?" Charlie began to read the caption: "'Father Christmas doesn't fail the children! Popular local figure Mr Ray Vincent, seen here with his daughter Amy, stepped into the breeches (literally) when a colleague was struck down with flu. Mr Vincent, past President of the society, took over the red robe rather than disappoint the children.'"

"It ties in with this report come in from Brisbane." Kev thrust it into his hand. "A woman passenger claims the man sat next to her talked about his daughter, Amy."

"Yeah, but Kev, this won't help identify him, not with the whiskers. Ah, that's better . . ." Charlie stared at the next photo, of a group of golfers. An arrow identified a fleshy-faced, fair haired man. "Looks as if Santa Claus has changed quite a bit from his visa mugshot."

Kev compared the one supplied by Immigration. "Clever bastard . . . just a few changes. This must've been taken when he was twenty pounds lighter, had more hair—"

"But why would Santa Claus need a 9mm pistol?"

"He was headed in the right direction." Kev stabbed the Brisbane report. "Could've been there, waiting for when the coaches drove into Wilcannia. Just his bad luck the seed packet wasn't on one of them."

"He picked the right coach, too," Charlie pointed out. "She and Pringle travelled with Pete. Do we know for certain why the engine was playing up?"

"Not yet," said Kev. "We're going to have to assume . . ." And Charlie nodded.

"Until we hear different, I'd say it's Santa."

There was a strangled cry from across the room. Both men turned. Anthony Pelham-Walker was clutching a signal and holding the desk for support. "I've been—dismissed!"

"Aw well, Pelham—" Kev tried to make it sympathetic "—it was a risk you took, comin' out here when it wasn't your problem."

"You don't understand—I must get back at once!"

"They're not likely to stop your pension, are they?"

"The honours list!" It was a moan from the heart. Charlie didn't understand.

"He's frightened he won't get a gong," Kev explained. "Listen Pelham, stick with us, mate. We can't leave you here, you'd be marooned. If anything's gonna happen, it's got to be during the next three days. Besides, when we get to Ayers Rock, that's where you can catch a plane."

Sixty kilometres out of Alice Springs, an old truck was parked within a circle of termites' nests, a straggling insect-made Stonehenge, each hollow segment nearly five foot tall.

Ray Vincent had spent six hours in Alice. He'd checked into a hotel, showered, then visited a bank. It set his teeth on edge when he had to do that—he hated leaving any traces—but he needed money. He'd bought the truck for cash; it was battered but it was adequate. He'd driven this far into the bush, checking his compass constantly, because he needed to disappear.

The heat was frightening. Would the tyres last? He'd only got three spares and the thorns between the rocks were needle sharp.

141

He forced himself to leave the car and pace several metres in each direction to check his isolation. Once he was satisfied, he rested. The driving cabin was an oven. He wrapped his sleeping-bag round his head for more protection. He was dehydrating as he sat there, but on this job you went by the clock; he wasn't due for the next sip of water.

The Heckler & Koch P9S was reassembled and inside the binoculars case. He'd taken the spring, screw and remaining metal parts out of the handles of his overnight bag after the last airport X-ray machine. When he'd killed the Bignell woman, he'd ditch the pistol altogether. It was too much of a risk to smuggle it back into England.

He slit open the cigars and loaded the training bullets; they didn't give the right "feel" but he didn't want to waste live ammunition. Now that he was ready, he allowed himself a sip of water before measuring out the range.

Powdery brown dust covered his trainers. When he stumbled, Ray Vincent deliberately wiped his hands on his shorts. He'd had to become a businessman again in Alice Springs but by the time he got to Ayers Rock, he wanted to be back inside the role of an ageing drop-out. People went out of their way to avoid bums, from middle-class indignation.

Vincent jammed the target in the bole of a ghost gum. The plate, ten inches in diameter, had been taken from the hotel where he'd rested for those few hours. He strode back to the twigs at the fifty-metre mark, hefting the gun from hand to hand, letting the strength and power filter through his nerves to his brain. It was irksome having only two magazines but more would've been risky. He'd allowed himself more time for target practice, to compensate.

He reached the mark. Without a pause, pushing the slide home as he spun round, he aimed at the device in the centre of the plate, "Telford Territory Motor Inn".

The plastic bullets gave no recoil. He emptied both magazines then waited, listening for the slightest disturbance in the surrounding bush. A pair of galahs rose and flapped lazily away. Silence. Ray Vincent walked forward to examine the plate, and immediately felt sick. It was cracked, that was all. He'd caught it twice on the rim, two out of thirteen, and only three days left!

If the scenery that day reminded Mrs Bignell of Mars, her first view of Coober Pedy was completely lunar. The vast Pimba plains had been empty of trees. Brown earth and scrub gave way to reddish dirt with yet more tufts of spinifex, but as they approached the town they could see not a trace of green, simply piles of shale, craters with mysterious ventilation shafts growing out of the sides, and ramshackle entrances opening on flights of steps that led underground; Coober Pedy sat astride undiscovered layers of opal.

They circled the low hills, some topped with shanty-type houses, until they came to a halt in a dusty open square. Opposite was what to Mr Pringle looked remarkably like a blockhouse.

"Sorry, folks. It's too windy to risk the tents." The FONEs stared at the billowing grey clouds. Dust had seeped inside the coach, they could taste it on their skin. "Sorry about the lack of a motel, too. They're plannin' on buildin' one here sometime. Meanwhile, they got this alternative accommodation . . ." and Lenny gestured across the square.

It was worse than any squaddies' hut, half tunnelled out of a disused mine, with double-tier metal bunks less than a foot apart. As shrieks of dismay began, Charlie looked round satisfied; he couldn't have planned it better himself. Only one narrow entrance? The seed packet would be snug and safe in here all night.

Amid the wailing and disbelief, Jean Protheroe's voice was loudest. "First you kill the family pet, now you reduce me to this!" As she paused to draw breath, Lenny said innocently, "Did you know they sell opals? The shop's in the cave over there."

Mavis didn't join the frenzied rush; she shook the nearest metal frame. "It's only for one night," said Mr Pringle encouragingly. One of the springs pinged and rust spattered on a spiders' nest below. "I don't think those can be the dangerous variety, at least I hope not."

"It's not the creepy-crawlies," Mavis said flatly, "even if they are twice as big as those at home; it's these bed-frames. None of them are up to my weight. And we'll all be in here together!"

"How about a little something from the shop?"

They walked along a passage hewn out of sandstone, breathing cool clean air gratefully. Lights glinted on quartz crystals still embedded in the rock. At a crossroads, branching galleries led in several directions, to coffee and souvenir shops, to wooden front doors with brass handles. "They really do live underground." Mavis was amazed.

"Not surprising when you consider the outside temperature."

"I wonder if Gary is behind one of those doors?"

The jewellery shop was doing a roaring trade in *bijoux* peace-offerings following the disastrous camp at Broken Hill. But what about tonight? Mr Pringle wondered. Would the world's leading scientists cope any better in a Stalag?

He saw with surprise that Mrs Bignell was by an open showcase. Ahead of her, Mrs Piggybum and her mate were already being served. Mr Pringle knew a desperate man when he saw one. "You've never worn jewellery before, Jessie!" the mate quavered; and she answered sharply, "No, because you're always too mean to give me any." Protheroe's quest for a suitable nuclear waste site was, Mr Pringle decided, producing an unexpected fall-out.

He came to attention. It was Mavis's turn and the assistant offered her a ring which she slid on her finger. "What d'you think?" He thought it very large but dared not say so.

"How about the dark one with the red sparkle in the middle?" It was much, much smaller. The assistant gazed in respectful admiration.

"Isn't it the most wonderful stone? They only find black opal like that once in a lifetime."

Oh my goodness! And he'd invited Mavis to try it on! Would they accept his pension book by way of a deposit? Mrs Bignell lifted the fiery perfection from its velvet bed. It stuck—it wouldn't go over her knuckle! Glory be!

"We can have it altered," the girl was saying. "When d'you leave?"

"Tomorrow, first thing in the morning," he gabbled. Mavis put the ring back and sighed.

"I shouldn't be tempting myself in here at all. What I'm really looking for in Coober Pedy is a Pom called Gary," she told the girl, "a long-distance driver. You haven't come across him, by any chance?" The girl relocked the showcase.

"Have you asked at the church? There's over forty nationalities in this town. They come and they go but most visit the church sooner or later."

Outside it was already dusk; the wind had died and in the stillness, Lenny was describing the wonders of the night sky.

"That's Betelgeuse. And Orion—on its side from your point of view. Tomorrow, at Ayers Rock, it'll be marvellous. Not many lights to dazzle your eyes."

"We know our way around the heavens," Protheroe began pompously.

"Yeah but d'you know what's beneath them as well?" Lenny shifted dust with the toe of his boot. "Under that, for instance?"

"More rock of course."

"Deep down, there's water. Enough to make the desert fertile. But if we pump too much out, we'll damage the whole ecological cycle for ever."

"Every schoolboy knows that!"

"What I'm getting at, is that you want to dump radioactive muck down there. Down the old mine-shafts. I heard you discussing it on the coach today."

"It'll be perfectly safe! Encased in glass and concrete designed to withstand hundreds of years—"

"If the stuff's so bloody safe, go stick it down a pit in your own backyard!"

Mr Pringle and Mavis sat for a minute or two; silence was instinctive. The church was another empty dug-out at the end of a tunnel. A few rows of folding chairs faced a cavity in the rock containing a wooden hitching post that was the altar. Behind that, a thumbstick with a horizontal branch made the cross. Decoration was the most primitive Christian sign of all, the fish, carved on the rockface behind the cross. After all the dust and heat, the church was an oasis.

Only one other person was there. Mavis stirred and spoke quietly into the void, "Is it difficult to find someone in Coober Pedy?"

"Depends if he wants to be found." The man considered Mavis

145

before adding, "Quite a few come here to get escape, for various reasons. Nobody asks questions."

"It's not personal, it's on behalf of a friend of mine."

Mr Pringle waited patiently as she went through the rigmarole. Was this stranger a priest or a sinner seeking forgiveness? There was no way of telling.

"Did the boy write this himself?" The stranger's question broke through his reverie; it was the same the friendly woman had asked on their first day in Bathurst. Mr Pringle leaned forward. "What makes you say that?"

The stranger explained. "The writing on this postcard, the shape of the letters . . ."

Of course!

When the stranger had finished looking at the photographs and handed them back, it was obvious what his occupation was. "If you find the father, tell him to bring the boy here. We have services for the sick. There have been cures."

In the last bar they found in Coober Pedy, the bartender looked faintly interested before he returned the picture of Gary. "Had a Pom in here a while back . . . couldn't get a job. He was a driver."

"It's as bad here as it is back home," Mavis said indignantly.

"Took him on for a coupla days. He paid for his tucker cleaning out the bar. Used to sleep in the corner over there. Quiet sort of fella."

"Was his name Gary?" The bartender shrugged.

"Who knows? No one asks in Coober Pedy. Ain't that sort of town."

Later, in the lower bunk, Mr Pringle wondered apprehensively if anything would befall him during the night? No other lady loomed as dangerously or as low.

His brain was racing now; it had been dulled by the heat but the stranger in the church had provided the necessary stimulus. The same doubt that had been at the back of Mr Pringle's mind, echoed by the friendly woman in the ice-cream parlour, provided the key.

He listed the questions he needed to ask Mrs Bignell tomorrow morning. When he knew the answer to those, they might be a little nearer finding Ben.

At least it had taken his mind off drug trafficking. And with FONEs in every bunk, the squalid blockhouse was a solid, impregnable mass of human discomfort. Mavis would be quite safe tonight; even the spiders had fled.

Chapter Seventeen

The level of water in the second plastic container was low but not dangerously so. Ray Vincent had marked off the hours on a stick with the same precision as the intervals between target practice. He varied the range, from fifty down to twenty-five metres, and his success rate had improved.

Sunset would soon be over. He moved quickly, making a rough bed of blankets inside the truck. The days when he'd learned to be a survivor out in the dark were long gone. He was soft with too much good living and the heat had sapped his energy, more than he'd anticipated. That killing affected him, too. He tried to shut it out but it was there whenever he closed his eyes—and it frightened him every time to remember how much he'd enjoyed it!

He'd been disgusted by Parker's behaviour but it was no use pretending—that surge of excitement had been just like the first time.

For Christ's sake, stop imagining things! It was a job, that was all, a job and nothing else. Let your mind rip like that and you were trapped in a circle with no beginning and no end. Pointless. Ray Vincent looked at his watch: time to eat.

He had kept his memory in separate compartments, ever since the first time. He'd been thirteen years old. Last night, Pandora's box had sprung open throwing out swirling kaleidoscopic violence. What had loosened the tight control? It frightened Ray Vincent that he couldn't understand when all he wanted to do was try and forget.

During the night he'd heard death screams from unknown creatures. Beneath his feet the ground pulsated with life that burrowed away from the sun. Animals and reptiles fighting both the heat and each other. Vincent wanted to be back in familiar terrain; he'd grown too old for this game.

Perhaps that's why forbidden thoughts returned to disturb him? Of the first time he'd watched human life disappear in a rattle of breath. He'd never forgotten it, just shut it away. Last night it came back; he'd had to relive each frozen second. Only then, when the memory was complete, could he sleep; it was always the same.

When he'd met Adele he'd tried to erase the past. After Amy was born, he'd made even greater efforts but it hadn't worked. Last night he'd experienced the same elation he'd known at thirteen—the feeling of absolute power that had blood pounding and intoxicated the senses—and he'd surrendered to it! That supreme moment when you knew you had stamped out life for ever. Despite Parker's brutality that feeling had consumed him when Evan Jones's eyes turned dull.

There was no excitement now, nothing but weariness. Ray Vincent had one chance left, that was all. There'd been too many mistakes and nowhere to hide. New York provided identities, passports, credit cards, supplied the cash and called the shots. He was forever their creature and the world wasn't big enough once you made mistakes.

He ate quickly, spacing out food with sips of fruit juice. He was filthy and the stubble on his chin was caked with dust. The only relief was an icy aerosol spray each time he changed his clothes.

Tomorrow he'd bury his dirty ones with the rest of the debris, before heading south down the highway. It meant a dawn start to be at the tourist resort near Ayers Rock by early afternoon.

The FONEs were due there in the evening. They'd be travelling north. According to their itinerary, they were due to stay two days; ample for his purpose.

He was fixing up an insect net when a movement caught his eye. For a few seconds, Ray Vincent held his breath. Softly, he slid a hand into the map compartment and reached for the gun. In a second he'd eased up the catch, pushed home the slide and fired.

It was perfect. He responded automatically to the recoil. No need to waste a second shot, he'd hit the target. In the fading dusk he bent down to examine it closely.

What had been a living creature was splattered over a wide area. This time Vincent hadn't used a plastic bullet but one from Zee's box, copper-jacketed, hollow-point, designed to mushroom on impact with flesh, and with a velocity of twelve hundred feet per second and sufficient power to kill a stag.

He'd blasted the tiny creature apart. From the head, he tried to gauge the size. The delicate pink lizard had scroll-like folds of flesh round its grey eye. Ray Vincent measured from the centre of the skull to the tip of the elongated nose with his finger. Say about nineteen centimetres overall. Like the gun in his hand, it was a perfect design, honed by billions of years of evolution to play its part in this harsh land; a beautiful, living creature. He'd hit it from, say, twenty-six metres? Not bad. Ray Vincent returned to the truck knowing he would sleep.

He woke with a start: Amy. No, he must not think about her until it was over—but he caught sight of his watch. Of the date on his watch. Back home it was Amy's seventh birthday. Christ! He'd forgotten it was today!

He'd never done that before—never been away on any of her previous birthdays. He'd got to find a phone, to tell her he loved her. Adele would never forgive him if he didn't.

After Coober Pedy, Yulara tourist resort would be heaven, the FONEs declared. How civilized to be in a tent once more! And with two days to explore Ayers Rock. Nothing to beat the rock, Lenny declared, nothing in the whole wide bloody world. Mr Pringle was inclined to think it might be true.

There was another reason why he and Mrs Bignell rejoiced: today it was their turn in the front seat. What bliss to contemplate the endless highway stretching ahead and watch vistas unfold. On a practical level, it also meant the Protheroes were at the back of the coach alongside the toilet.

Mavis was more than ready to admit she'd grown tired of Kenneth Protheroe. "I don't know how Jean puts up with it, day after day."

"Perhaps she's fond of him?"

"No, I don't think so. Not after what he did to the rabbit." She was in her floral blouse and fuchsia skirt, in honour of the occasion, and wore the tiny opal studs Mr Pringle had presented to her at breakfast.

"A small consolation because we didn't find Gary."

"They're lovely," she told him. "Let's face it, we didn't really expect to. That Pommie driver in Coober Pedy turned out to be called Gareth, with a wife in Liverpool, did I tell you?"

Lenny climbed into the driving seat and saw the flowery profusion. "My word!" Mavis blossomed.

"It's going to be a lovely day, I can feel it in my bones. Rather hot, I expect, but you can't have everything, can you?"

They turned off the main highway and began heading west. Here, views became much more green, trees, bushes, even the scrub, but the earth itself was red. Where growth was sparse the ground was ochre colour, but beneath the shade of Casuarina trees it become red as blood. Ahead, gouged out of the land, the carefully graded dirt-road stretched to infinity.

Suddenly, to the left and framed by trees, a solid dark shape appeared on the skyline. Protheroe couldn't contain himself. He raced to the front of the coach, camera at the ready, fat bottom blocking the view, deaf to everyone's protests.

Lenny waited until the roll of film was finished. "Got what you wanted?" he asked cynically.

"Magnificent, thanks!" Protheroe turned to face his colleagues. "Some of you may not know, Ayers Rock is a boulder, separate from the earth's crust," he lectured, "and like an iceberg, the greater part of it is buried beneath the sands of the desert."

"Don't you think you'd better wait until we get there?" Lenny sounded laconic.

"Pardon?"

"That ain't Ayers, that's only a little rock, Mount Conner. 'Bout another thirty kilometres before we gets a glimpse of the biggie."

Golly, thought Mr Pringle, if that was "little", what on earth was the other one like?

In the Yulara resort a short distance from the rock, a dusty Toyota and an old truck arrived within minutes of one another. In the Toyota, two men were arguing. "Look, Pelham, I don't want to share a tent any more than you do—"

"I fail to comprehend why we cannot spend the night in an hotel."

"I told you, there's a conference goin' on at the Sheraton." Kev indicated the dusky rose-coloured building with high-tech aluminium sails to protect it from the heat. "They've got delegates from forty countries. Plenty of headaches for security and the police. They can't spare anyone to help out. Which means until somethin' breaks, it's down to you, me and Charlie. Now let's have a beer and get the tent up."

In the Visitors' Centre, the grubby figure looked out of place. Ray Vincent was itching to be outside, merging with the mixtures of types and nationalities on one of the campsites. In this elegantly cool interior, flanked by screens and arrangements of grasses, he was conspicuous. "Can I help you?"

"I want to make a long-distance call." He spoke quietly but it was still too loud. Other visitors might pretend to be deaf, that was all. They weren't travel-stained as he was but he daren't waste time in a shower. Already Amy would be in bed, probably crying herself to sleep because he'd forgotten.

He had to restrain himself from hurrying across to the Perspex dome. He seized the receiver. "Hi, Adele? Wake the birthday girl up, tell her Pop wants to give her a great big kiss."

"Ray . . . is that you?"

Despite the thousands of miles, he was there beside her in the room. He could see her face. He knew what had happened. "What's wrong?" He didn't have to ask because he knew. He had to hear her say the words. Until she did, it wasn't real.

"What's happened?" It was difficult to breathe, to keep his voice steady. When Adele spoke, the words would be printed in his brain for ever and he would share her agony.

"Where is she, Ray?" The voice was a tired shadow from hours of weeping. "They said you would know. I've been waiting . . . I haven't been to the police. They said Amy would be killed if I did that . . . Who are they, Ray? Who's Parker? What have they done with my baby?"

The terror was so great his body hunched tight to stop himself screaming. "It's all right, Adele . . . promise. They'll bring her back . . . As soon as I've done what they want . . . It'll be all right . . . Darling, I love you!"

He shouldn't have said that. Anger and fear burst from her in one great wave of hate that swamped and choked him so that he put out a hand to stop himself being knocked over by it. When he tried to speak, he found she'd rung off.

Mavis spotted it first. This time there was no mistake. The most massive rock she'd ever seen in a vast flat plain. Huge though it was, that rock had turned on its side in a prehistoric ocean, back in the Dreamtime.

"It's incredible," she whispered.

"Yep," said Lenny fondly. "That's it, that's the biggie."

"Are we stopping?"

"Not right now," he replied. "I want to show you the Olgas first."

"If they're bigger than that," Mr Pringle protested. "I don't think I can cope."

"The Olgas are a group of boulders. None of them's larger than Ayers but together they are. The black fellas have the same sort of beliefs about them. The Olgas are part of their legends but I don't find them as spooky."

"You're right," said Mavis slowly. "Ayers has an atmosphere, even from here. It's very powerful."

"That's what the black fellas say. It's their place of mysteries." Pete glanced in his mirror at Protheroe, back on his feet to re-establish his superiority. "It's been here since the Dawntime, according to them. I hope it lasts a while longer."

"Surely no one would interfere—" Mr Pringle saw his glance and understood the implication. "Oh, dear . . . let us hope not."

The Olgas were half an hour away across the desert. In the clear late afternoon light they saw the huge features of the Dying Kangaroo Man, as the Aborigines dubbed him millions of years ago. The stone glowed dark red, sculpted by nature and full of pain. Even the scientists fell silent at the sight of it.

At the foot of the Olgas, like ants they scurried about in an effort to come to terms with the phenomenon. For Mr Pringle, each vast stone had been weathered in curves so that the whole took on the form of a slumbering female megalith, awaiting the call of her god.

It was a relief to be offered fruit squash; to climb back into the protection of the coach. For Lenny insisted they return for the greatest experience of all: the few precious moments when Ayers Rock comes alive with all the colours of the setting sun.

When it was over, Mavis couldn't find words to describe it. They were at the campsite at Yulara and she watched Mr Pringle rig their tent. "I'd no idea it would be like that . . . that article didn't prepare you at all . . . Would you like me to give you a hand, dear?"

"No thank you." Mrs Bignell's efforts with guy-ropes were well-meant but lacked cohesion.

"Red, purple, blue . . . and over so quickly. Kenneth Protheroe didn't get the film in his camera. I heard Jean shouting at him. 'All this way,' she was yelling, 'and you manage to miss it!'"

"I fear his has not been a particularly successful trip. What are the plans for this evening?"

"After we've eaten, the coach will take us to where the pubs are. That's where the truck drivers go as well as everyone else."

Yulara had been built twenty kilometres away from Ayers Rock in a scooped out depression of the land and carefully landscaped. Linked by a drive, the area contained hotels, camping areas separated by hummocks, a swimming pool, shops, visitors' centre and an amphitheatre.

In the middle and tall enough to screen even the hotels, was a lookout from which everyone could gaze his fill at the rock.

As he climbed to the top to look at the view, Mr Pringle decided the complex was the best answer yet to the problem of tourism. Buildings were a dusky ochre to blend with the desert. Each had the same futuristic aluminium sails, strung above the roofs to deflect the sun. Very little would be visible outside the area, he decided.

He caught a glimpse of the thatched roofs of an earlier settlement much nearer the rock. Too near, he thought. This was one place on earth where Man should respect God's mysteries.

He remembered with a start he was supposed to be protecting Mrs Bignell. There were still some questions to be answered, too. On the coach, she'd refused to be distracted from the sights.

She was unpacking inside the tent. Charlie squatted near by, inflating the airbeds. Mr Pringle nodded to him and crawled

154

through the flap. "About Mrs Hardie's son—" he began.

"Oh, not again, dear! I told you all I knew this morning. He died before I met Mrs Hardie and she doesn't like talking about it."

"His death was not entirely unexpected?"

"I don't think so, no . . . like I said, she goes out of her way to avoid mentioning it. And I never pry."

"Of course not," Mr Pringle paused to let the ruffled feathers settle. "In the photographs on her mantelpiece, I noticed how much Ben and his uncle resemble one another."

"Yes," Mavis agreed. "It's the blue eyes, I think, it makes the whites so clear."

"What about ill-health? Was Mrs Hardie's son prone to sickness?" She considered.

"I'm not sure, dear. As I say, I can't remember her talking about it."

"But when Mrs Hardie's son died, was there an inquest?" This time she was truly shocked.

"Are you suggesting that my friend, Mrs Hardie—"

"I suggest nothing. Can you answer my question?"

"If there'd been any hanky-panky we'd have heard about it at The Bricklayers," Mavis said firmly and turned her back on him. Mr Pringle retreated.

Outside, the sandy soil was blood-red under the lamps. It seeped between his toes. Back on the knoll he looked at the distant black mass of the rock and, near at hand, the resort with the line of the drive picked out in arc-lights.

He watched a bus make the circuit of the drive, picking up passengers. There were other coach parties and families in camper vans, tents dotted about and tourists sleeping in their cars. Everywhere lights twinkled among the trees.

As Mr Pringle turned for a final look at the rock, he saw a shape on the edge of the ridge. It was near enough to make his blood run cold. When it howled, he gave a nervous involuntary yelp.

In the dark, the dingo brought to the surface all the disquietude; he was in an alien land, in a desert beside a primordial rock. What was worse, there were unknown dangers threatening Mrs Bignell but she still refused to go to the police. "Tomorrow," she'd promised, "as soon as that letter's in the post."

Suddenly there were other dogs silhouetted on the ridge; the pack was assembling, drawn by the aroma of so many barbecues. Mr Pringle experienced an acute desire for human company and hurried back down towards the tents.

"Guess you're not used to this kinda life, Pelham?"

"At home, the climate is unsuitable."

"Yeah . . . we keep everythin' ready in the garage. At weekends, we just fill up the Esky and go where the fancy takes us. It's the great outdoors all right. The kids love it."

"Fiona and I decided against having children."

You would, you mean old poofter, thought Kev. Catch you wanting to share . . . He flipped the steaks on the griddle and walloped on chilli sauce with a lavish hand; proper man's food.

Anthony Pelham-Walker watched in irritation. There was surely no need for all this nonsense—why not take a table at the Sheraton and eat in a civilized manner?

He made no attempt to help clear away either but waited for the main business to begin. Kev spread out the papers from Macquarie Street. "Now . . . let's sum up what we know so far."

They were opposite the tents that housed the FONEs. Kev had pitched theirs so that surveillance was a simple matter. Charlie would watch from the other side where he, too, had an unimpeded view.

Kev sorted telexes into neat piles. "According to immigration, Vincent has blue–grey eyes, height five-ten. Seems he's visited five times during the last six years. Occupation: Estate Agent. Home address: Farnham, in the county of Surrey. Wife: Adele . . . married seven years, one child, Amy. That's all."

"Apart from a 9mm pistol."

"Yeah . . . even out here, real estate ain't that rough. What've you got?"

"According to Sinclair, Vincent set up the agency, apparently from scratch, five years ago. He provided all the capital himself. His previous occupation was listed as 'Security Adviser'."

"Covers a lotta possibilities, Pelham." Kev pulled the tag off another can of beer. "Anythin' else?"

"Sinclair has had difficulty tracing anything more than seven or eight years previously. Vincent bought his present house—again for cash—on the outskirts of Farnham and joined various clubs in the area, presumably to establish himself in the community."

"He'd just got married," Kev pointed out. "What sort of a place is this Farnham, in the county of etc?"

"An old market town, increasingly occupied by London commuters of a high-earning capacity. Houses are pricey."

"So about seven years ago, this bloke appears with his new wife . . . and plenty of cash. The dates tie in with the increase in traffic our end, when the organization really got started and we had the first big surge. Heroin was available all over the place. Did Sinclair come up with anything about the second mystery man who killed Evan Jones?"

"I fear not. It's not his field."

"Yeah . . . another desk fella."

Anthony Pelham-Walker ignored him and stared at the photographs. "It's possible the second man is here also, having evaded Immigration's watchdogs. Have you had these circulated?"

"Yep—and it is possible," Kev agreed. "If so, you, me and Charlie might be in for some nasty shocks the next coupla days." Pelham-Walker swallowed. "However . . . as this Vincent character is our only lead—because according to Macquarie Street no one else has connected him with a job—I suggest we concentrate on him. *Someone* has to contact the Bignell lady and relieve her of those two packages."

He picked up the Brisbane report once more. "Passenger confirms male subject, early forties, wearing heavy glasses, etc, etc . . ." He skimmed through the rest. "Remarks of special interest: subject uses perfumed unguent and referred to daughter 'Amy' in affectionate manner." He tossed the report across. "If it was Vincent, he's slippin'."

He folded his arms in a manner that was now familiar to Pelham-Walker. "Why would an old ex-pro who's losin' his grip come all this way? Why not use an operative based here?"

"Perhaps because he's personally responsible?" suggested Pelham-Walker.

"Could be, Pelham . . . So where's he hidin'? What d'you think?

Is our man in the Sheraton over there, getting ready to make his move?"

If he is, thought Anthony Pelham-Walker bitterly, it was thoroughly unjust.

In a lean-to made from groundsheets strung between ropes attached to the truck, Ray Vincent lay between his blankets.

Sleep was impossible: Parker had Amy. It was his only thought and it burned a hole in his brain. Nothing else mattered except what Parker might be doing, just for the hell of it. Parker who'd wielded that hammer . . . who'd laughed so excitedly. What would Parker begin to do to a seven-year-old girl?

It had to be tomorrow. He daren't waste more time. He would phone New York and demand that Parker release her, he'd risk another call to Adele, he'd catch the first plane to New York if that's the price they demanded, but please God, let Amy still be safe!

That morning there was another postcard from Mavis and a brown envelope from the DHSS. Mrs Hardie limped back to the kitchen and opened the envelope first. A form confirmed the allocation of sheltered accommodation and gave a date two weeks hence when Mrs Hardie could expect to move in. Underneath, the welfare lady had scribbled a message urging her to let Linda know "at the earliest opportunity".

Nothing like the present, Mrs Hardie thought shakily. She'd make the tea first. Maybe she'd be strong enough after a nice hot cuppa.

Linda was bleary-eyed. She drank thirstily from the vulgar mug. These days she scarcely bothered to greet her mother in the mornings. It was the booze, Mrs Hardie realized that. Linda spent most evenings at the pub. According to the home help, there were empty bottles in the dustbin. Gin and Campari, that's what this daughter of hers drank. Proper alcoholic's brew that was. Mrs Hardie put the DHSS form on the worktop. "I've had this today."

"What?" Linda drank her tea and stared out of the window.

"It's confirmation of a place. I've accepted this time. You'll not stop me whatever you say. I've told the welfare it's definite." Linda turned away from the window and refocused on her mother.

"What are you on about?"

"If you ring and ask, they'll tell you what's available. You'll have to move, this is family accommodation. The welfare lady's expecting you to call. I said I thought you'd want two bedrooms . . ." Mrs Hardie's voice and courage faltered.

"I'm not moving because of Ben. You know that. We've been over it hundreds of times!" Linda was already shouting and her mother backed away.

"Linda, he's not coming back. Gary won't let him go, you know he won't. Even if Mavis manages to find them—"

"I'm not moving from this house!"

The shriek stunned Mrs Hardie. When she recovered, she said quietly, "You'll have to, Linda. They won't let you stay on. You haven't got enough priority. There's another family due to move in here—"

"No!" Linda had her mother by the shoulders, shaking her, forcing her to understand, "I'm not . . . leaving . . . !" The metal crutches crashed to the floor. Mrs Hardie clung to the worktop.

Her daughter's face was inches away from her own. She couldn't escape the staring, pleading eyes. Linda was willing her to understand. Mrs Hardie shrank away, the stale breath adding to her sick fear.

"I'm not leaving, Mother . . . Ever. Because of . . ." Linda hesitated, looking past her mother at photographs on the mantelpiece.

Mrs Hardie seized the pause. "Because of what, Linda? What are you trying to tell me?"

Eyelids drooped over the protuberant eyes. Everything about her daughter was suddenly flaccid. When she spoke, she was exhausted.

"You know. You're running away because you've no guts . . . but it's your fault as much as it's mine."

This time, Mrs Hardie shut her eyes.

As the moon rose, they howled; every dingo in the pack adding to the hideous, mean wailing. In their tent, at the end of the line, it was unnerving. Mrs Bignell snuggled up, warm and curvaceous, and reached out a hand. Mr Pringle's hopes were immediately raised. "That emergency haversack of yours, dear. . . ?"

"Yes?"

"You haven't got a tin of Mr Dog in there by any chance? One or two sound as if they could do with a nibble."

Chapter Eighteen

In the cool of the early morning, Mrs Bignell vanished into the laundry room of the shower block and Mr Pringle obediently hoisted a washing line. It was a time for pottering, for catching up with postcards, posting Evan's letter and visiting the police.

To his surprise, Mavis had capitulated without further argument. "We'll find a pillar box then the police station. I expect they've got one in the Visitors' Centre—although I doubt whether the police here will be interested. They'll probably insist we go to the ones in Sydney on our way back home."

"Possibly. But it will be a relief to tell someone. Look at this newspaper, the report of some Customs haul in the UK, nothing to do with us but it mentions the street value of one drug." He indicated the Australian headline.

" 'Heroin valued at £200,000 a kilo!' " Mavis was incredulous.

"You see why I'm so anxious, if that's what it was?"

"Yes, I do . . . How wicked . . . two hundred thousand pounds." It made her very thoughtful as she gathered her bits and pieces for washing.

Mr Pringle began a solitary breakfast. None of the FONEs were about. Charlie went past on his way to have a shower. Apart from that, Mr Pringle was alone in the dining area. From the other side of the camping lot, screened by the Toyota, Kev watched him through binoculars.

"Mind if I join you?" asked Lenny.

"Please do." Mr Pringle waited until he'd pulled up a stool. "I was beginning to wonder where everyone was."

"Sulkin' in their tents."

"Oh?"

"Yeah . . . seems like there was an altercation at the Sheraton last night," Lenny drawled. "Protheroe organized another of his

161

meetin's—'Extending the hand of friendship and profit'. Invited anyone who was interested to learn how much profit could be made out of nuclear waste."

"What went wrong, weren't they interested?"

"Too right they was interested!" Lenny waved the piece of sausage on his fork. "Over at that hotel there's a conference goin' on. International CND. There're representatives from forty different countries havin' a pow-wow 'bout the Nuclear Menace. They turned up and they was very, very interested. There was what you might call an exchange of ideas."

"Oh, dear!"

"Them FONEs looked sick as parrots by the time they got back last night. All the same—" Lenny looked along the line of tents "—they can't stay sulkin' in there. They'll fry when the sun gets up. My word, look at that!"

Mrs Bignell had returned and was pinning up her washing. Fluttering in the breeze it sent an exotic signal that warmed cockles deep inside Mr Pringle; silk and satin underwear in lavender, purple, whisper-pink and pearl, the message was unmistakable, utterly feminine and inviting.

"My word!" said Lenny again. "Them's her campin' frillies?"

"Oh, yes." Mr Pringle felt like a sultan. "My friend doesn't believe in lowering her standards because we're in a desert."

"You two comin' on the trip to the rock? Coach leaves at ten-thirty 'stead of two o'clock. I thought it'd be better than climbin' in the heat."

Oh bother, thought Mr Pringle. Mavis came across, all fresh and sparkling in her marigold outfit. Lenny explained the change of plan.

"I don't suppose it'll matter, will it," she asked expressively, "if we post that letter this afternoon?"

"But we're not going to put off—the other matter?" Lenny had gone for toast and marmalade but Mr Pringle remained cautious.

"As soon as possible," Mavis agreed. "As soon as we get back from the rock, we'll go and tell them."

Anthony Pelham-Walker had been detailed to be a messenger-boy. He hadn't been ordered about like this since he was a fag. It made him very angry but Kev insisted. He trailed back wearily from the Centre and flopped down beside the Toyota.

"Aw, there you are, Pelham. Breakfast's nearly ready." Macillvenny was doing it deliberately, he thought: bacon, sausage, tomatoes, fried bread and a slithery fried egg to top the lot. "Now, what's the news this mornin'? Anything happened back there?"

"I made those enquiries you suggested," he replied stiffly. "No more telexes from Sydney. However, long-distance calls made via the operator yesterday included three to England."

"And?" But Anthony Pelham-Walker didn't work as speedily as that.

"I have my address book." He produced it from his blazer pocket. "Fortunately one of my wife's relatives lives in Aldershot which is next door to Farnham . . . the codes may be similar."

Kev's chewing slowed then stopped. Pelham-Walker's finger fumbled down the page. "Yes, here we are . . . the Beresford-Smiths. How odd." He looked up, surprised. "I think we must assume the caller *was* ringing Farnham. One of these three has a code which is precisely the same—0252—it's a most unlikely coincidence someone else would be calling Aldershot."

"Most unlikely . . ." Kev agreed. "Vincent's here, all right. It's got to be him. The bastard's somewhere on this site—and he's come for the stuff!"

Mrs Piggybum was doing her hair, winding the grey plait round her head and stabbing home the hairpins. Once it had been a thick blonde tress that had had Porky boy in paroxysms. In those far-off days she'd been his little "Swiss miss". Porky boy had changed, much to her regret, he'd become stringy and grey, like her coiffure.

She'd never altered her style, she still wore dirndl skirts. Not now of course, not in the desert. For this holiday she had trousers, bought from Help the Aged, shapeless and comfortable.

Mrs Piggybum had seen the exotic flags on the washing line, fluttering shamelessly. It caused indignation and pain inside the shrivelled academic chest to think that Mrs Bignell could even afford such garments. Expensive scraps of satin and lace—what about her moral obligation to the Third World!

All the same . . . curiosity got the better of Mrs Piggybum. Seeing no one about, she approached the washing with discretion.

It was difficult to judge who had the greater shock. As the man emerged abruptly through the tent flap, Mrs Piggybum squealed. He was nothing better than a tramp! "What d'you think you're doing? That tent doesn't belong to you!" Strong, upper-class, and no-nonsense.

"I was hoping to find Mavis Bignell." Clipped and just as authoritative.

"You'll probably find her—"

"What are the plans for the day? Are you going to the rock?" The questions were rapped out and she answered instinctively.

"Some of them are. The coach leaves at half-past ten. Who shall I say was asking. . . ?" But the man was striding away. Typically Australian, no manners whatsoever.

Still in a huff, Mrs Piggybum resumed her quest. Like every other woman—and several of the men, come to that—she had an overwhelming desire to know the exact size of the brassière . . . Damn! She wasn't wearing her glasses.

Anthony Pelham-Walker resigned himself to his final day in the appalling heat. The first connecting flight was tomorrow and, by God, he'd be on it. He ignored the excited chatter between Kev and Charlie. This business had nothing more to do with him, he should never have got involved.

But what was the point in rushing home? His job had gone, his chance of glory. If life had been pointless before, he'd made it doubly so by coming here and losing any hope of a title.

That was the only reason Fiona had stuck by him. She'd probably consulted the most expensive divorce lawyer in London by now—one who would suck him dry. What a prospect! Disgrace and poverty, all because he'd imagined his life meaningless!

Mrs Bignell had her sunshade as well as her dark glasses. The coach wasn't full because some of the FONEs had decided to go swimming instead. As they drove, she kept remembering the newspaper headline. "Those two bags . . . four hundred thousand pounds!"

"Try not to worry. We'll go to the police first thing this afternoon. About Mrs Hardie's son, Billy . . ."

"Yes, dear?"

"Can you remember any reference she made? She must've talked about him occasionally." Mavis frowned.

"I think she told me once he was better off dead, something like that. She was upset. She was crying when she said it." Mr Pringle looked grave. It was a judgement he'd learned to mistrust.

"Those photographs she has; Ben resembles Billy in several respects. They have the same vivid blue-white eyes, their limbs are thin. In fact, one could say Billy too looked as though he might have had rickets as a child." Mavis sighed.

"I know what you mean, they were both bandy-legged. I never knew Billy but Ben was almost deformed. Like Tweedledum because his legs were thin sticks supporting his body. He had a terrible time at school, poor little soul."

"And Billy died when he was how old? A teenager, in his early twenties?"

"Yes but *Ben* hasn't died," Mavis protested. "He's had one or two accidents, that's all." Mr Pringle frowned.

"There are similarities, nevertheless."

Lenny leaned across from the driving seat. "You weren't planning on climbing the rock, were you Mavis?"

"No, dear. I shall sit at the bottom and admire Mr Pringle." She squeezed his hand. "He's going right to the top!"

"Do you consider I am attempting too much?" Mr Pringle was nervous. This morning Ayers looked twice as big as it had before. Lenny glanced at his shoes.

"Those got good soles?"

"Oh, yes. Very sturdy. And I have my pack." He was proud of his haversack; it had weathered the five decades since his scouting days pretty well. "Water bottle, first aid pack, signalling flare. . ." Lenny raised his eyebrows.

"Have you a sweater?" he asked. "It may be ninety out there now but when we get to the top, it gets real windy." Mrs Bignell made him open the haversack and show her his woolly.

"I knew I could rely on you, dear, but I just wanted to be sure."

"Funny thing about the rock," Lenny mused. "It gets to people. They find it strange . . . outside their experience. Some of 'em get dizzy up there. It's the view. There you are, on top of the world, and there's nuthin' whichever way you look, 'cept the Olgas . . . and Mount Connors. Miles and miles of empty space. That's what does it. People fall off."

"Oh, my Lord!" Now he'd really upset Mavis.

"I shall take great care," Mr Pringle assured her. "I shan't venture near the edge on any account."

"They put brass plaques up." Lenny wanted to comfort them with authority's concern. "Everyone that fell off, there's a plaque with his name and the date on it . . . five of 'em, so far. I tell people, make sure the next one isn't yours."

He flicked on the mike and spoke to the other passengers. "We're makin' a detour, folks, round the old holiday village. This is where tourists used to stay but they stopped usin' it after that business with the dingo and the baby, right?"

Heads nodded up and down the coach.

"The black fellas live here now . . . and one of the rangers—they look after the religious sites and whatnot—he's a mate of mine. Thought you wouldn't mind if I stopped to say hello. Won't take five minutes."

They turned on to a dirt-track in the shadow of the rock. Here, scrub and thorn were already clawing back the shacks. As they approached, Mrs Bignell got her first real sight of the Aborigines. Black faces, some with incongruously fair hair above the jet skin. Faces with *retroussé* noses that would have been pert but for the hopelessness in their eyes.

Women sat with their backs to the trees, in the shade; lassitude emanated from them. Children played in the dust. Men stood and waited to see what this day would bring. There was a feeling of resignation as well as inevitability that was disturbing. This ghost of a white man's holiday village was now inhabited by the dispossessed. "What do they do?" asked Mavis. "Living here?"

"Not a lot," Lenny replied. "They don't have to work. Most of 'em don't particularly want to. This is their bit of territory, the rock. Much of it belongs to them now. They like it here. Right, here we go . . ."

He pulled up beside a thatched hut, in better repair than most, and called "Anyone home?"

In the coach, Mrs Bignell was unnerved by the silence of the watching blacks. Lenny had left the coach door open. Like one or two of the party, she descended and walked towards a group of children, uncertain for once how to greet them. "Hallo . . ." None of them answered. Lenny ducked his head and went into the hut. He came out smartly.

"My word, he's got problems."

"Oh?" Mr Pringle was casual as he descended from the coach.

"White ants . . . place is swarming with them. Guess that's why my mate's decided to move out for a while . . . He's taken his things. Hang on a minute. I want to find out where he's gone." Lenny walked over to the watching black men. One of them recognized him. Immediately the atmosphere relaxed and greetings became friendly.

"Have you got a bit of string in your haversack?" Mavis asked Mr Pringle.

"Yes, of course." He handed it to her. She put down bag and parasol and began a cat's cradle. The children watched, silent, impassive. After a few minutes, one indicated Mrs Bignell should give the string to him. He tied it to a stick as a whip and began flailing the others.

"Oh well . . . you can't win them all, can you dear?"

One of the girls disappeared inside a hut and brought out a home-made toy, two rusty cans linked with string, knotted at either end to make a primitive telephone.

Mrs Bignell accepted a can with delight, checked it for ants and held it to her ear, pulling the string taut. "Come on then, send me a message . . ." There was a bout of giggling among the children. None had the courage to begin. Mr Pringle took the can and spoke into it.

"Burr . . . burr . . . burr . . . burr . . ." he said solemnly. "Hello? Can anyone hear me?" More giggles but another child made as if to listen. "Burr . . . burr . . . burr!" he cried, much encouraged. On the other side of the dusty square, a man had joined the group round Lenny. The movement attracted her attention and Mrs Bignell glanced across. The next minute she began to wave vigorously. "Look, dear, look—it's him! Ooh-hoo!" She lifted her parasol and twirled it high. "Gary! It's me . . . Mavis, from The Bricklayers."

Dust rose in flurries as, both hands outstretched, Mrs Bignell hurried across, full of the pleasure of finding him. FONEs and Aborigines alike saw first Gary's disbelief then his astonished laughter.

On his side of the square, Mr Pringle realized what had happened. "Lines to the rest of the world are engaged," he announced hurriedly, "please try later," and handed back his receiver.

He walked more slowly, not wanting to interrupt the first precious moments, but very conscious of the heat through his straw hat. Mrs Bignell was bursting with happiness and as he arrived, turned to introduce him. "This is Mr Pringle who's come with me to Australia. Gary's living here, dear, above the garage. He's working as a mechanic with the Aborigines." She turned back, full of happy anticipation. "Now, Gary, tell me, how's Ben?"

It was as though she'd extinguished a vital spark. Gary stuttered but couldn't speak. Mr Pringle murmured a politeness to fill the embarrassed pause. It was a shock to see how much older Gary looked than the photographs.

Gary unfroze as though aware of the awkward situation. Lenny came to his rescue. "Look . . . it's too hot, folks. How about sittin' in the coach? I've got the fan on in there." Under her parasol, Mavis dabbed at her forehead.

"What a good idea . . . A few minutes and I've had enough. Can you spare the time to come with us, Gary? Some of our party are going to climb the rock but you and I can stay in the coach and chat."

After a brief word with the Aborigines, Gary followed as though compelled to by the presence of so many strangers. Mr Pringle sensed his complete reluctance. He stood back courteously for him to board the vehicle. Gary's expression was that of a man entering a trap. He made one effort to save himself.

"Look . . . my overalls are covered in grease . . . don't want to dirty the seats in here."

"That's all right, mate—" Lenny was amiable "—Got a toilet on board with soap and water. You can use that."

Gary stood motionless as though they'd taken away his last chance of escape. Mr Pringle waited. When he spoke, it was to mutter, "OK, I'll come."

The rest took their seats and Lenny started the engine. As the cool air built up, Mrs Bignell's energy returned and she began an animated account of Bricklayers' news. She made occasional references to Mrs Hardie and Gary's apprehension appeared to grow. He answered questions about work; it had been hard to find any on his return. When the money ran out, he'd had to turn his hand to anything, anywhere. He'd hitched lifts, away from towns where there were plenty of locals for every vacancy. He'd been employed as a janitor at the holiday complex when he'd heard of the need for a motor mechanic.

"Not many are willing to work alongside the black fellows. I don't mind." Gary hesitated as if seeking the right words. "They don't—interfere." Mrs Bignell didn't understand.

"About Ben, dear—" Gary stood abruptly.

"Guess I will go and clean up . . ." He hurried to the back of the coach. He looks ill, thought Mr Pringle. He cut through Mavis's surprise.

"May I suggest you avoid all mention of Ben, for the present."

"What an extraordinary thing to say!"

He knew it wouldn't satisfy her but he didn't understand himself, not yet. Finally he said, "I think we should go carefully. It might be to do with Billy," which annoyed her even more.

"Look dear, I'm not one for riddles."

"Would you say Gary looked pleased to see you?"

"At first, yes, of course he did. Why shouldn't he?"

"But when you asked about Ben?" Annoyance changed to alarm. "You don't think—something's wrong?"

"I'm not sure. Will you let me talk to Gary? In private?"

In the car-park at the base of the rock, the three of them sweated in the Toyota. "Lenny's takin' a bloody long time back at the village."

"He's catchin' up with an old mate," said Charlie. "Relax. There're all of them FONEs aboard. Vincent wouldn't attack in a place like that. Too public."

"It can't be worse than this," said Anthony Pelham-Walker irritably. "This is like Piccadilly on a bank holiday."

Tourists of every nationality walked past, some laden with climbing equipment, most in shorts and trainers. Beyond where their coaches were parked, an old pick-up truck pulled in and stopped.

"Here they come," said Kev suddenly. "Here's Lenny . . ." The Wallaby Tours coach swung past in a slow arc to park alongside the rest. "Hey, just a minute . . ." He focused his glasses. "Isn't that an extra passenger getting out?" He handed them to Charlie. "Quick, take a look; blue T-shirt and overalls. I haven't seen that one before."

"Nor me." Charlie stared at Kev. "Reckon we could've been wrong about Vincent?"

"Gary has very kindly agreed to accompany me on my climb," Mr Pringle told her. "You don't mind, do you, Mavis? Now that we're here, it's a little larger than I anticipated. I might require assistance to reach the top. You and he can have your chat when we return."

Privately, out of Gary's hearing, he whispered, "You gave him a shock, appearing out of the blue like that. I think it'll be all right once he's recovered."

"Yes of course. Thoughtless of me." Then, brightly, "Lenny's been telling me about the caves at the foot of the rock, where the Aborigines have their fertility rites. He's offered to show the rest of us."

"They don't go in for that sort of stuff nowadays," Lenny put in hastily. "It's all in the past. But there are wall paintings datin' back thousands of years. You need to know where it's OK to go. Some's forbidden because it's sacred ground. It offends the black fellas if you pry too close to those."

"Look after Mr Pringle for me, won't you Gary? See that he doesn't get blown over the edge."

The two followed the rest of their party across the soft sand, ochre colour in the harsh light, a deeper, richer red under the sparse tufts of porcupine grass. Sand flowed over their feet and burned through the soles of their shoes.

They reached the low outlying boulders that marked the beginning of the climb, letting the scientists go on ahead.

Lenny waited to see them all go then backed his coach out of the parking lot, turning right along the road at the base of the rock. Seconds later, the old truck did the same. In the Toyota there was a rapid debate.

"The seed-packet lady's stayin' on the coach!"

"Yeah, but look, Kev . . ." Charlie pointed excitedly at the haversack on the inoffensive back. "See what Pringle's carrying? There's more than two kilos of weight in that—and why's he actin' so friendly with a complete stranger?

"I've been tryin' to tell you 'bout how he behaved at Yunta—dashing across the road as soon as a stranger talks to the seed packet—he knows about the stuff all right, he must do. Either *she* told him or he's been in on the deal from the start, who knows? What the hell! Pringle's carrying more than two kilos on his back and he's with a contact!"

"Yeah but it's not Vincent!" Kev was adjusting his binoculars frantically. "He's too skinny, he's got dark hair—"

"He could've dyed it for Chrissake!"

"But what about the seed packet!"

"What about her? She's on the coach with no one but the FONEs and Lenny? We saw her get on this morning—she wasn't carrying more'n a purse and that brolly thing," Charlie insisted urgently. "But up there, disappearing by the minute, is Pringle with a fella we haven't seen before."

"OK, we don't know for sure that it should be Vincent. And where the two of 'em are goin', there's loads of places you can be private."

"Right! C'm on, Kev, it's got to be the contact. Couldn't be anyone else."

"OK." Kev made his decision. "Let's go."

Charlie leapt out and flung open the boot, throwing a camera at the astonished Pelham-Walker. "But why go up the goddam rock?" Kev asked obstinately. "When there's millions of square miles of nuthin', why go to all that trouble?"

"I dunno!" Charlie answered sharply. "All I do know is I can see them with my own eyes, going up, up, up—and if we want to get a shot of the exchange, we'd better decide pretty damn soon. Quick, Pelham, on your feet."

"I? You're surely not suggesting—"

"*We* is goin' up there, all three of us. Me and Kev to take care of the contact—you to photograph the exchange, now *c'm on!*"

Gary had paused so that Mr Pringle could read the notice at the foot of the rocks. " 'Prepared mentally and physically?' " He was brought up short by the implication.

"Yes," Gary nodded. "That's the way to describe it. You'll find out. Go in front, I'll follow. Rest whenever you feel you have to, especially on the chain. And don't look down until there's room to sit and rest."

"You don't mind accompanying me?" Mr Pringle asked, a little shyly. "It was partly a ruse, I'm afraid, to escape Mrs Bignell's eagerness. Now that we're here, I don't mind admitting I welcome your companionship."

Gary smiled, the first untroubled smile since they'd met. "I'd guessed the reason. But I don't mind, honestly. At the top, it's the most peaceful place I know." He was about to add something but changed his mind, and they began the climb.

It was smooth where Mr Pringle rested his hand, weathered by sun and wind since before the Dreamtime, and by the ocean on which the rock had once floated. Sun had dried up any lichen. Ridges banded the surface in parallel curves that looked as if they continued for ever, down through the red sand to where the rest of the rock lay hidden; uninterrupted ridges, seven kilometres long.

How vast was the unknown portion? It was another of the mysteries and swamped Mr Pringle's imagination. That there should be more than this immensity was unnerving. A tiny human ant, he concentrated on putting one foot in front of the other. Already it was becoming steep. He could see the first of the iron posts ahead and beyond it, the chain that was the handhold over the steepest part; if he could only reach that, he would allow himself the luxury of a rest.

*

Between the road and the entrance to the caves there were bushes and scrub. The rest of the passengers came to a decision. "We'll wait," they told Lenny. "We'll be quite comfortable here until you two get back."

He and Mavis had to push their way through bushes and he grew concerned about her dress. "There's always been water here, that's why there's so much growth. See the marks where it gushes out of the rock? After there's been a wet, of course. They call it Maggie Springs here." Mrs Bignell took a few deep breaths and dabbed on eau-de-Cologne.

"I've never had a spring named after me but they do call it Mavis's bar in The Bricklayers."

"You know, I think I may pay a visit one day. Your pub sounds real nice."

"You'd be most welcome," said Mavis hospitably, "but try not to make it a Thursday: We sometimes get a rude class of person on Thursday nights. I always discourage Mr Pringle from coming round then because it upsets him."

"I'll remember," said Lenny. "Now, in here—mind your head—this is what they call the Hunters' Cave. There's some paintings of animals right behind this stone."

He crouched down and so did she, intent on the bright, primitive outlines, protected by the boulder from the sun. Behind them, someone slipped unnoticed into the cave.

"See the shape of the bird?"

"Oh, yes . . . like an emu. And what's that, a crocodile?"

"Move!"

"I beg your pardon?" Mavis, startled, looked at Lenny. He reacted slowly, too slowly for the vicious kick that thrust him into the dirt. Even as Mavis opened her mouth to scream, the butt of the pistol thudded down on his unprotected neck. Ray Vincent continued the swing, hitting Mavis hard with the edge of his hand.

"Where is it, where's the stuff?"

She closed her mouth and jaw, dizzy with pain.

"It's not in the tent—what've you done with it!"

"If you want my handbag, take it." Her voice was muffled but she managed to cry out as she saw him about to strike again. "Take it, I'm not stopping you!"

He thrust something cold into her face. "Those two bags? You got five seconds." Genuine bewilderment mixed with terror slowed Mrs Bignell's life to a standstill. It was ridiculous, a man with a gun? You only saw those on the television.

"Talk!"

"D'you mean the powder that Evan—?"

"Where is it!" His whisper hissed round the cave. Without thinking, in agony from the barrel pressed into her eye, she whimpered, "I gave them to Mr Pringle—"

He should've fired but he didn't, he hit her instead, slamming the pistol against her skull.

As he drove away, the image of her—red hair, red blood—merged with Amy's face, Amy with a knife at her throat and behind Amy, Parker. Laughing.

A cloud of dust covered his car, fine, powdery and deepest red. The sand under his feet as he ran was the colour of blood. He pushed his way past groups of Dutch and Japanese tourists and began the ascent. The sun burned down out of an empty sky and the rock burned red with the heat.

They'd taken frequent rests for which Mr Pringle was extremely grateful. Gary was a kind young man, very considerate. A face so much thinner than the photographs. Hair no longer dark but mixed with grey and with bleak, sad eyes.

They'd avoided discussion but each of them knew it couldn't be postponed indefinitely.

About half-way up, for no apparent reason, Mr Pringle said, "I was talking to Mrs Bignell about Billy. She wasn't able to tell me much." Gary looked at him.

"You know?"

"No. I made the connection. More than that . . . a lack of necessary medical knowledge." He shrugged.

"I knew Billy, you know," said Gary. "When we were kids we used to play together. But I never guessed. And they never let on, Linda nor her mother." Gary was trying to make him understand, he realized that. He caught various phrases above the wind and began to put the whole together.

It took an hour to reach the top and when they'd got there it was so tremendous he could think of nothing else. It was impossible to be anything but exhilarated. This was the summit of the world, God's not man's; with a bird's-eye view of a continent. He and Gary stood on a plateau. Mr Pringle wanted to whoop and shout but the wind tore the sounds away. He staggered like a crazy man until Gary stopped him. In the end, exhausted, he sank into a hollow in the rock.

"Oh good gracious . . . I never expected it would be so marvellous. Oh, I must take another look . . . I can't just sit here!" He was wobbling about, drunk with the view, the sun and the wind. His legs gave way a second time and Gary hauled him back into the hollow.

"Take it easy . . . it's been there for billions of years, you can risk another half-hour."

"Yes, I'm so sorry . . . how foolish."

It was strange; being on top of the world had taken away fear and brought him to an Olympian realm detached from everyday reality. He couldn't put it off any longer.

"I have to tell you, Gary, at first I thought Ben was ill. I thought you'd brought him here because of the climate . . . then I remembered the pictures of Billy. Ben's uncle. The same features, the same—illness?" He felt rather than saw the nod.

"I decided it must be hereditary. Lack of knowledge made me wonder about haemophilia but there the joints are swollen. Ben's limbs were emaciated." There were tears in Gary's eyes and they weren't caused by the wind.

"I do not pass judgement," Mr Pringle said softly, "I've never had a child—but is Ben dead?"

"Yes . . ." It wasn't loud but Mr Pringle heard it.

"You never brought him to Australia?"

Gary shook his head. Inside Mr Pringle a coldness began that he knew the sun couldn't warm. He forced himself to ask, "If you didn't bring him. . . ?"

"We did it together, me and Linda."

"Ah." He didn't want to move, he was too old and cold. Instead he let Gary talk.

"There wasn't a cure, even out here. I sent a couple of letters and a postcard so Linda's mum would think I'd got Ben."

"Yes." And two people had recognized that a child hadn't written it.

"Ben was like Billy. Worse. Linda knew—before she had him, she knew." Livid anger, controlled until now, burst out of Gary. "She kidded me about it but she knew. Because of her brother. Her mother was a carrier, it ran in the family; Linda wouldn't have tests because of that."

"What was it, that Billy and Ben had?"

"Osteogenesis imperfecta." Gary managed a sad smile. "They're the only big words I know . . . Got the doctor to write them down so I could learn them."

"They're beyond me, I fear. What do they mean?"

Gary reached inside his jacket, taking care that the gusts didn't whip the contents out of his hand.

"I think this could be it . . ." Kev had the binoculars now. He was on a lower ledge, braced against the wind and in danger of losing his balance. He took no notice of the scruffy, stocky figure scrambling up below. "The contact is taking something out of his pocket . . . handing it to Pringle—could be the cash—Pringle's looking at it closely! Get a shot of it, Pelham!"

"I'm in an extremely dangerous position because of the overhang—there's no possible way I can take a photograph—"

"Get the other side, Charlie, quick! Hold on to Pelham while he gets those pictures!"

Below, Ray Vincent caught sight of them. He veered away, on a route that would bring him round the edge of the plateau, to the opposite side from the two sheltering in the hollow in the centre.

"Pringle's taken it. He doesn't seem surprised." Astonished, then angry, Kev said, "Whatever it is, the bloody fool's looking at it closely."

"Give me the glasses, let me see!" Pelham-Walker's sudden desire to participate nearly sent Kev off his perch.

"Watch it!"

Charlie began inching forward on his belly, to a higher rock,

176

slightly above and over twenty metres distant from Pringle and his contact, but if either man stood up they would see him.

On the opposite side, Ray Vincent moved forward, hand over hand clinging to the rock below the edge. Beneath him the void was so deep it made him sweat. His hands were wet. As his grip slipped, the strap of the binoculars case ran down his arm to his wrist and swung to and fro in space. He could feel the gun banging about inside. Closing his eyes he pressed his body against the rock, lifted the strap over his head and eased the case round to lie in the small of his back.

Over three hundred metres below, a dot that was an ambulance moved away from the caves and began the return journey to Yulara.

Chapter Nineteen

The two men, sheltered from sun and wind, sat with the few pathetic mementoes of a life. "They remind me why I did it," Gary said simply.

The photographs had been handled so often, wept over so many times, the stains were a part of them, but sorrow wasn't enough. "I thought I'd get over it. You never do. I know that now."

"No." Mr Pringle had meant what he said earlier, he was neither judge nor jury, but he needed to understand. He picked up the first photograph. "One woman suggested Ben had rickets."

"No, it was the disease. Those words mean imperfect bone development. Ben was born with fractured legs. By the time he'd begun to crawl, they looked like that."

These weren't bland snapshots, they'd been taken deliberately to show the nature of the illness. "See this one? Ben's first day at school, on calipers. He was back home by dinner-time. He'd dislocated his arm." Gary relived the bitterness. "We lost count of the number of fractures in the end: arms, legs, ribs—his bones were too soft and they'd never be anything else. There was no way he could grow up to be normal. And there was pain every time he broke a bone. Ben wasn't spared that."

"No." Mr Pringle had another picture. "I can see it in his face." Ben's stunted puny body in a hospital cot with traction applied to both limbs. The eyes with their blue-white fringing, dark with apprehension. "What were they trying to do here?"

"Insert nails into his bones. They'd broken his legs on purpose that time, to try and straighten them. It didn't work. He was such a brave kid . . ." Tears were falling now. "I used to sit beside him in that hospital, willing him to take my strength, holding his hand through the worst of it . . ." Gary turned away to recover and Mr

Pringle waited. Up here they weren't god-like after all, they couldn't shed their burdens.

"I knew by then we shouldn't have had children." Gary's voice was rougher now. "I got one of the doctors to explain. She wrote down the words for me, admitted there wasn't a cure . . . 'Some day,' she said. 'Just hang on, for Ben's sake.' Only I couldn't.

"When I got home that night I shouted the words over and over again at Linda. She knew all right. She'd always known. I should've killed her, not Ben, to stop her having any more."

"Nevertheless, what happened . . . what you did to Ben was murder."

Tired eyes acknowledged it to be true, but Gary didn't speak. "What do you intend to do now?" Mr Pringle asked sadly. "You can't run away from it for ever."

"Stay here." Gary was defiant. "The black fellas know. I told them. They see it differently. They don't think I did wrong, they understand. I loved Ben!" he shouted. "He'd got nothing to live for. He'd got it so bad all they could do was keep breaking his little bones, hoping they'd grow straight next time. Every day he was in pain! It was going to take years for him to die, years of pain! I did it the kindest way, you've got to believe that, while he was asleep. He didn't wake up, that's all. That night, Ben stayed asleep."

Gary rocked to and fro. "We buried him . . . We had to do it that night. Linda's mother was away, the neighbours were on holiday—"

"You don't mean Ben's still there!" Mr Pringle was horrified.

"What else could we do? Linda told everyone the rockery was her idea. I left her to get on with it. Never went back. I couldn't stand any more of it."

"Oh, Lord . . ." Mr Pringle felt old again. "Ben deserves a Christian burial, Gary—"

"What good will that do?" Gary was on his feet. "Will it bring him back? Stop the pain? It might make *you* feel better if they lock me up. No, I'm staying. They accept me here."

"Somethin's happening," Kev called quietly. "They're on the move."

179

Spread-eagled on the red-hot slab Charlie murmured, "About bloody time."

Anthony Pelham-Walker had the binoculars but could no longer make things out. Shimmering heat distorted the outlines. He was light-headed from the sun on the back of his neck. The wind elated him; he knew if he cast himself off it could bear him up like an eagle. He swept the glasses over the plateau—and saw the face!

Ray Vincent was impatient. He couldn't manoeuvre in this confined niche. He'd waited long enough.

He hated looking down but there in the distance was the head of the climb and below, the stanchions supporting the safety chain. There was no other way down. He couldn't see the three on the opposite side but it didn't make sense for them to be there still, not in the heat, so where they hell were they?

There were blisters on the backs of both his hands, his skin was almost too hot to touch. Much more of this and he'd pass out! He checked the descent one last time; not a soul, either climbing up or going down. The three men must've gone down while he was clinging on for dear life, making his way round the rock face; he hadn't dared look down then!

He heaved himself up. Pringle and his companion were still in their hollow. Pringle was on his knees, unfastening his old-fashioned haversack. Christ, was he about to hand over the stuff? Who the hell was the other chap? He'd have to go, too. There couldn't be any witnesses.

There was the flash of sun on glass. Vincent instantly dropped back into his niche—careful! Pringle's spectacles must have caught the light. Give it a few more seconds, to make sure neither of them were looking in this direction. The second hand crawled round the dial, twenty-nine . . . thirty . . . a last check of the other two then placing both hands flat, he levered himself up on to the edge of the plateau.

"At least have a drink," Mr Pringle was saying. "We're both tired after that climb and there's no need to go down until we're feeling calmer. I took the precaution of bringing a bottle of water."

He was reaching for it when Pelham-Walker made his move. This was the opportunity he'd been waiting for; his life would have a meaning after all! He had to get there first, to haul Ray Vincent from his hiding place, before Macillvenny did. He flung the binoculars aside, leapt on to the plateau and was off.

Mr Pringle and Gary turned to see a stranger hurtling towards them as though his life depended on it. Behind him, a much larger man appeared and lumbered in pursuit.

It was most extraordinary.

From farther back, behind the first two, a third, tough-looking younger chap jumped down from a slab, pulling at something tucked in his belt.

Gary cried, "Look out! That one's got a gun!"

"Pardon?"

And Gary fell on him, pushing him flat.

Anthony Pelham-Walker was running too fast to stop. As Pringle and the stranger dived, he saw Ray Vincent face to face for the first time, crouched above the edge, arms fully extended: in his hands he, too, had a gun.

Ray Vincent couldn't retreat, behind and beneath him was the void. He screamed and shouted but the wild-eyed fool kept on coming, blocking his view of the two in the hollow. Anthony Pelham-Walker was less than two metres from him when Vincent fired twice, at the target beyond.

Closing the gap and with his gun in his hand, Charlie tripped and fired simultaneously.

The corpse, one hollow-point bullet mushrooming to maximum devastation inside, changed its trajectory. There was sufficient impetus to carry it forward as gravity took over. Ray Vincent ducked but one of the outspread arms caught in the strap of his binoculars case. The jerk halted the downward flight and the body hung there momentarily, spiralling in space. For several seconds, Vincent tried to rid himself of the dead-weight, clinging to the rock with terrified, sweaty hands, but the nylon webbing was strong, and Anthony Pelham-Walker completed his mission.

181

Chapter Twenty

In the Yulara medical unit, the sister said caustically, "Oh, she'll live. First thing she asked when she regained consciousness was 'Do they have male nurses in Australia?' "

"She's out of immediate danger, I take it?"

"You can see her for five minutes, that's all. At her age, whatever lies she tells about it, nature has to take its course. She's still suffering from shock and it's too soon for her to have visitors."

Mr Pringle crept into the cool room. The face on the pillow was so badly swollen, he wanted to weep. Only the familiar titian strands escaping from the bandages confirmed it was Mavis. He touched her hands and she opened her one good eye. "Hello, dear . . . are you all right?"

"Yes."

"I thought he was a mugger at first . . . but he wasn't. Did you tell him you'd got rid of the stuff?"

"There was no need."

"Poor Evan. Fancy being mixed up with people like that."

"Don't worry about that now."

"How's Lenny? He kicked him so hard, then he hit him—"

"Lenny is recovering. He'll be all right."

"What's going to happen tomorrow? Will they leave us behind?"

Mr Pringle pulled his weary senses together and put the terrible events from his mind. "Another driver is taking Lenny and the FONEs back to Sydney. We're to stay on here and return with Pete when he's well enough. He'll travel down from Alice Springs and collect us. You'll be here about four or five days, according to Sister."

"Lenny suggested we might like to visit Darwin. He says there's a very nice pub there, the Vic."

"It's nearly two thousand kilometres to Darwin!"

"How about the barrier reef? Can we pop over there instead? I could wear my costume."

"That would be even further." Mavis shrugged then winced.

"It is a big place, isn't it, Australia? That article didn't give you any idea . . . Never mind, we found Gary. Has he said yet how Ben is?"

"Try and sleep. Sister said you were to rest as much as possible—" but Mavis had seen the parcel.

"What have you got there?"

"Oh—yes." He was reluctant. "The ladies in the party, Mrs Protheroe and, er, Mrs Piggybum—her name is Wilkinson, by the way—when they heard of the attack, they thought, in view of the shock, you might need a warmer nightgown."

He shook out the folded garment and Mavis inspected it with the bloodshot eye.

"My God, I wouldn't wear that as a shroud!"

"No. I thought as much." He shook his head over the hideous colour. Large buttons restricted access at every aperture. "I believe Mrs Wilkinson donated it herself . . ."

"I've often wondered who wore things like that." Mavis's croak was strong suddenly. "Now I know." The eye swivelled round. "You can tell them from me, it's the thought that counts, all right?"

"Yes." There must be a polite way of expressing it but he was blessed if he could think of one.

They had lifted Gary and Charlie off the rock by helicopter and taken them to Alice Springs. Mr Pringle had watched until it was out of sight. For several minutes, he stared at the edge where one man had toppled on top of the other and dragged him over. The second had screamed and screamed and then disappeared, the wind mercifully bearing all other sounds away.

Someone had led him back down, taking all the time in the world. Mr Pringle thought it kind but Kev Macillvenny knew there was no need to hurry. At the foot of the rock, Kev sat him in the Toyota and tried to explain what had happened.

One word made sense. "Oh, the drugs! The packets that Evan Jones. . . ?"

"Exactly," said Kev. "All you got to do is tell us what you've done with them."

And Mr Pringle admitted to the manslaughter of Sydney harbour seagulls. As Kev and Charlie agreed afterwards, with that old-fashioned sort of a Pom, it couldn't have happened any other way.

In Men's Surgical in Alice Springs, Pete was feeling better. He began to take an interest in his neighbours, especially as one of them, surprisingly, was Charlie. With a heavily bandaged foot, Pete was sympathetic. "Hope you fixed the bloke that did that?" The sister overheard.

"Go on. Tell him what happened."

"Go to hell!"

"He did it himself," she told Pete. "Just climbed to the top of Ayers Rock and shot himself through the foot. Comes from New South Wales, which might explain it."

It had taken all her strength. First the coach journey, then the difficulty of finding the address in London, but Mrs Jones had made up her mind she would do it. She stood outside the block of flats with the card in her hand. Number four. It was the right name beside the bellpush. She rang and waited. Crispin Sinclair's voice crackled through the answerphone, "Yes?"

"It's about . . . Evan Jones." She spoke so quietly he told her to repeat it.

"I need to—see you," she said urgently. When the buzzer went it took a moment before she realized the front door had been unlocked. She pushed it open and went upstairs, taking the kitchen knife from her bag.

He overpowered her but not before she'd stabbed him badly. As she explained first to the police, then the court, she wanted to hurt at least one of those responsible, because of what had happened to Evan.

On this occasion, press and television couldn't be muted by the department. Every savage detail was described. Torture and murder had resulted from a lack of concern on the part of the authorities, declared the magistrates. Crispin Sinclair considered it grossly unjust. Sacked, attacked, and now held solely responsible for a Welsh peasant's death.

The ultimate insult was that Batman should end up a hero!

Kev Macillvenny broke the small item of news himself.

" 'Fraid Gary passed away last night."

"Oh, no!" Mr Pringle cried out in distress. "I thought—they'd found the bullet and operated?" Kev shook his head.

"That bullet was vicious; it was designed to explode inside the body—the bastard who fired it knew that. It smashed Gary's spine and paralysed him. No future for a bloke like him, you know."

But he did it to save me, Mr Pringle wanted to shout; it was my fault that he died. Kev guessed his thoughts exactly.

"Look, mate, try and see it from another point of view. They let me talk to Gary yesterday. He knew by then he wasn't going to make it. I explained how that bullet and the one that killed Pelham were intended for you 'cause Vincent must've assumed you'd got the drugs.

"Gary didn't bear you any grudge. Can't speak for Pelham but he did what he did off his own bat. Must've recognized Vincent through the binoculars and decided to go for him. He knew Vincent was armed." Kev sighed over the stupidity. "Anyways, Gary told me all about that business with his kid. Said you were to tell Linda it was his fault. He reckoned if he took the blame, she'd be off the hook.

"I'll be sending a copy of his confession to the UK authorities, but Gary definitely wanted you to be the one to tell his ex-wife, OK?"

Mr Pringle nodded. It wasn't much in return for what Gary had done for him. Perhaps, when she was well enough, he could share the burden with Mrs Bignell. She would find words to help him bear it.

Kev sat, smug with pleasure, beside Charlie's bed. "Written your report yet?"

"No!"

"Keep your voice down or Sister'll get upset. Got to write it sooner or later, you know."

"OK, OK. What 'bout Pelham? What's happened 'bout him?"

Sun poured down on the mottled skin beneath the sparse hair. After a few days in the desert, Kev was beefy red. Talk of Whitehall made him clench his fists.

"Like you and me could've guessed. They were embarrassed by what Pelham did, right? They already sacked him—but what do they do now? They make him out to be a hero! It was on the TV last night." Kev attempted the sugary-solemn tones: " 'Regrettable mishap to British public servant attempting a civilian arrest on Ayers Rock.' "

Charlie said reluctantly, "Aw, c'mon Kev, Pelham was brave, you gotta admit that."

"He was bloody dumb! He was a gunny idiot to jump a man with a pistol pointing at his belly! Pelham got between Vincent and the target—"

"OK, OK . . . so what 'bout Mrs Pelham? Did you talk to her? Was she upset?"

"Nope." Kev's voice was neutral as he helped himself from the six-pack in the locker.

"What?" Charlie was shocked. "Not even a little bit?"

"What she said was—" Kev ripped the tab off a can "—when I told her Pelham fell off of Ayers Rock while tryin' to apprehend this dangerous British criminal . . . She said, '*Where* did you say all this took place?' " Kev imitated a supercilious voice this time. " 'Where on earth's that?' Then she said, 'Do you mean to tell me he's been in Awstraliah?' "

"You mean, she never knew Pelham was out here?" Charlie was incredulous. "He'd been gone over a week, an' she hadn't even noticed?"

"Maybe the butler forgot to tell her."

"Poor old bugger!"

"Yeah . . ." Kev paused to finish his beer before pronouncing the epitaph. "I never liked Pelham. He was the worst Pom I ever met but he ain't half saved the tax-payers some money . . ."

"An' Vincent?"

"They bin workin' hard in Macquarie Street," Kev admitted. "Traced the bullets—bought by a Chinese woman, would you believe?"

"Not another missionary!"

"They're checking it out. That telephone number Pelham recognized. Belongs to Mrs Vincent. The daughter was kidnapped a week ago."

"Christ! She's a goner, considerin' how he blew it," Charlie said flatly.

"Yep."

"So what about you and me, Kev? We collectin' a vote of thanks, or what?"

"Nope." Kev enumerated the reasons: "We ain't got evidence 'cause Pringle fed it to the birds, we lost our link with the organization 'cause he got yanked off the rock, and we lost a Pom who'd just bin sacked because Vincent shot him by mistake. But they ain't grateful in Whitehall. They sent a telex with two big words in it, Charlie." Kev rolled them round his tongue, "'Considerable ineptitude.' So . . ." He tossed the beer-can into the basket. "Comin' back to that report of yours, why not tell 'em the truth? Just say you was on Ayers Rock, and fell arse over tit and blew this great big hole in your foot?" He shrugged sadly. "It's what the Poms expect. It's what I bin warnin' you 'bout for years. Anyone who's dumb enough to wear them tight jeans—"

"Aw, shut up!"

On their last night in Sydney, Mavis insisted they watch the news, "To see what's been happening while we've been away." Mr Pringle could have wished that the first close-up hadn't been of Protheroe.

"A highly successful visit!" Mavis was outraged. "They practically threw those FONEs out of Australia!"

With his years of experience in the Revenue, Mr Pringle was able to present a different point of view.

"Protheroe has obviously been schooled by one of those failed television directors on how to handle the media. I came across quite a few in my last district."

"But the FONEs weren't successful!" Mrs Bignell insisted angrily.

"Ah, but that's part of the current work ethic: never admit to failure. What Protheroe is doing is an illustration of creative thinking. He is being economical with the Truth."

"Twaddle! It's a complete fabrication from start to finish."

"Alas . . . I fear falsehood isn't a word included in current vocabularies. It would be considered counterproductive, especially if it interfered with the facts." Mavis snorted.

"Talking of fibs, I've still got to phone Mrs Hardie. I can't put it off any longer."

"Wait until we're back in England," he begged.

"I'm sorry, dear, I've got to do it while I still have the courage."

But when she put down the receiver, she said quietly, "They've found Ben. Linda confessed. She didn't know about Gary admitting to it first. She's told the police it was all her idea."

Chapter Twenty-one

Mrs Bignell said she would go alone. Mrs Hardie would prefer it. He could come with her when she visited Carmarthen because that would be far more gruelling but not this time.

She and Mrs Hardie took a taxi to the cemetery. Her friend chattered throughout the short journey and led the way, apparently undisturbed, stopping occasionally to point out the features.

"They call this part the Children's Corner. It's better kept than some of it. See the way they've trained that rose across the arch? That's the entrance." Birdlike and trim she bobbed across wet earth. "You should have worn flat shoes," she called; then, "This is the place . . . this is where they've buried Ben."

It was a small mound among many, grassed over and featureless apart from the tablet:

BEN COLES, AGED 7 YEARS
"SUFFER THE LITTLE CHILDREN"

"They let Linda choose the words."

Mrs Bignell stooped and laid the small posy beside the stone. "I'm glad for your sake Linda admitted it in the end." Mrs Hardie nodded, head tilted in the familiar way.

"She thought I'd guessed, you know . . . We never talked about Billy, about him being . . . about the illness. It may sound stupid that I couldn't, Mavis, even after he'd died. When someone's like that because of what he got from you—you can't begin to describe what that's like.

"Anyway, when Linda told me she was pregnant, I kept hoping Ben would be—normal. It was unfair to Gary, wicked. But there was still a chance, you see. At least, Linda and me hoped there was."

Mrs Bignell took her friend's arm. Together they stood in silence at the foot of the grave.

"What happened to Gary? He didn't kill himself did he?" Mrs Hardie asked timidly.

"Oh no, dear, nothing like that." Mavis considered for a moment how to describe what Mr Pringle had told her, to avoid more upset for her friend.

How could you explain about men appearing from nowhere on top of that great rock and firing at one another, and Gary being shot instead of Mr Pringle, or so he claimed?

All because a misguided Welsh boy with nice manners had asked her to do a favour . . .

A dreadful thought began to take shape in Mrs Bignell's mind and swell to frightening proportions: it wasn't all *her* fault was it? She hadn't started it all those weeks ago when she'd first smiled at Evan on board the aircraft?

"It was an accident," she replied firmly. "Gary saved Mr Pringle's life but everything that happened, including Gary being shot, was accidental. Take my word for it."